"Damn, you'll... so damn spoiled with you. Get on me. I am ready for you to shovel coal into my furnace."

"Hell, Murty, you are always ready for loving." He rose on his knees and laughed. Coming between her raised legs spread wide, he shoved the nose of his erection inside her and she *ooh*ed out loud.

"Damn, you're like Old Faithful at Yellowstone, spouting off about every half hour!"

The next twenty minutes they were lost in each other's rapid response. Swirling around like some great whirlpool, they left the real world for one of passion and hellfire even the Yellowstone geyser could not match.

DON'T MISS THESE
ALL-ACTION WESTERN SERIES
FROM THE BERKLEY PUBLISHING GROUP

THE GUNSMITH by J. R. Roberts
Clint Adams was a legend among lawmen, outlaws, and ladies. They called him . . . the Gunsmith.

LONGARM by Tabor Evans
The popular long-running series about Deputy U.S. Marshal Custis Long—his life, his loves, his fight for justice.

SLOCUM by Jake Logan
Today's longest-running action Western. John Slocum rides a deadly trail of hot blood and cold steel.

BUSHWHACKERS by B. J. Lanagan
An action-packed series by the creators of Longarm! The rousing adventures of the most brutal gang of cutthroats ever assembled—Quantrill's Raiders.

DIAMONDBACK by Guy Brewer
Dex Yancey is Diamondback, a Southern gentleman turned con man when his brother cheats him out of the family fortune. Ladies love him. Gamblers hate him. But nobody pulls one over on Dex . . .

WILDGUN by Jack Hanson
The blazing adventures of mountain man Will Barlow—from the creators of Longarm!

TEXAS TRACKER by Tom Calhoun
J.T. Law: the most relentless—and dangerous—manhunter in all Texas. Where sheriffs and posses fail, he's the best man to bring in the most vicious outlaws—for a price.

JAKE LOGAN

SLOCUM AND THE KANSAS SLAUGHTER

JOVE BOOKS, NEW YORK

THE BERKLEY PUBLISHING GROUP
Published by the Penguin Group
Penguin Group (USA) LLC
375 Hudson Street, New York, New York 10014

USA • Canada • UK • Ireland • Australia • New Zealand • India • South Africa • China

penguin.com

A Penguin Random House Company

SLOCUM AND THE KANSAS SLAUGHTER

A Jove Book / published by arrangement with the author

Jove Books are published by The Berkley Publishing Group.
JOVE® is a registered trademark of Penguin Group (USA) LLC.
The "J" design is a trademark of Penguin Group (USA) LLC.

For information, address: The Berkley Publishing Group,
a division of Penguin Group (USA) LLC,
375 Hudson Street, New York, New York 10014.

ISBN: 978-0-515-15438-2

PUBLISHING HISTORY
Jove mass-market edition / March 2014

PRINTED IN THE UNITED STATES OF AMERICA

10 9 8 7 6 5 4 3 2 1

Cover illustration by Sergio Giovine.

1

There was nothing but brown grass waving on the wind-swept rises. The Kansas sun glared off the swaying stems and seed heads that did their thing like great ocean swells. A dull blue sky held no break of even a small cloud from horizon to horizon, and the air was filled with the squeak of cart axles and the stench of the green buffalo hides that were stacked in the wagons behind him.

Slocum reined up his gray horse and held his hand up to halt the train at the sight of three corpses. Pinned down on the ground side by side were the naked, mutilated bodies of two white men and one white woman. Loose strands of wavy blond hair were blown by the wind across the woman's ashen face.

He dismounted, then quickly turned and caught the thick-set young woman running toward them with her dress's hem barely reaching her knees.

"No, Murty. It's too damn bad for you to look at." His body, clad in a fringed buckskin jacket, became a shield to keep her from seeing the heinous slaughter.

1

"Them red bastards killed more white folks? That's it, ain't it?" Wrestling with her trying to get by him was about more than he could stand.

"Yeah, they did more of their bloodletting. Goddamn it! Don't fight with me, woman." It was like wrestling with a bear. She was strong as any man from all her work cooking, doing chores, staking out hides, and throwing them in the carts and wagon. He could have fought one of the men easier. At last he slipped his arms under her armpits and, with his hands clamped behind her braids, forced her to walk back to her wagon and mules, with her cussing and crying at him the whole time.

When she was at her mule teams, he whispered in her ear, "Stop this goddamn fussing with me or I'll bust your ass."

Her finger was in his face. "I got my rights!"

"To stay here. Now, build a fire. We're going to give them a civil funeral. You make supper."

She acted like she'd throw a block at him if she had one, and then went to where she damn well pleased to stomp her foot. Finally, she turned, straightened her breasts under the dress, and acting still mad, went for her kettles and fire makings. "You can't go ordering me around like I'm your slave either, Slocum."

"I know. I know. Lincoln turned them all out."

In Spanish, he shouted, "Escatar, Juan, Leo, get some shovels and get up front. We're having a funeral for those less fortunate."

"*Sí, Patrón,*" they shouted and rushed to the front to join him.

"Dig a deep grave. One the wolves cannot dig up to eat them." His Spanish words drew nods from the men. They knew what would be required.

He drew his bowie knife and knelt by the first man—he had no name for him. About thirty, he had a row of numbers tattooed on his right arm. Poor son of a bitch had served time in a war prison camp, only to later be gelded in his last hours on the earth by rabid red men. Slocum sliced the buffalo leather ropes on the man's feet and then pulled the first of the stakes driven through his palms. The stakes were like the nails the Roman soldiers drove through Jesus's hands.

That was done while these men were still alive. He fought the victim's hand off the first stake and put his arm by his side. Then did the next limb. In an instant he saw the gray horse looking off to the west. He jumped up to see what the horse saw out there in the distance. In response to the column's approach, he jerked his buffalo gun out of the scabbard.

"What is it?" Escatar asked.

"Riders."

"Guns," his Mexican *segundo* shouted to the others. Then he ran fleet-footed to tell the others back with the rigs and animals. "Guns. Guns. Get ready."

"I've got mine," Murty shouted at him. "Who in the hell is it?"

"Look west yourself. All I can see are riders." Slocum bent over to cut the blond woman's legs loose; then, when he stood again, a sour knot came up behind his tongue. What a waste. A beautiful girl maybe eighteen and butchered. They had only tied her wrists to stakes—he cut them loose too.

"I don't think they are Indians, *Patrón*." His foreman indicated the column, rejoining him.

"Good. Dig some more."

He used his brass telescope to peer at the column. They were not military either. Though they rode two abreast like a cavalry did. A big man who acted like a general rode beside the bearer of a strange flag. It was neither Mexican nor American.

Slocum freed the other man's hands from the stakes and then cut his legs loose. He rolled the bodies over until they were close together, then he covered them with an old blanket his men had brought him and put dirt on it so the wind did not blow it off them.

The hole's progress deepened.

Murty came with her yellow hammer Winchester. "What do they want?"

And she indicated with her gun barrel the column approaching them. "Kind of spooky. Them ain't nothing I ever seed before."

"Go cook your food. Be dark soon and you'll be bitching I didn't give you enough notice."

She looked at the blanket over the dead. "How many?"

"Two men and one pretty blond woman."

With a shake of her head, she went back, with the rifle ready in her hand.

He heard her tell one of the men she passed when he asked her something, "How in the fuck should I know? He don't."

The grave was deep enough.

An emissary with a white flag, who rode a fine sorrel horse, came at a gallop. He slid the horse to a stop.

"Colonel Bradford wishes to speak to you."

Slocum stood with his .50-caliber Sharps in the crook of his arm. His wide-brim beaver hat still shaded his eyes. "Tell him to get his ass up here. We ain't got all night."

"Were some of your people killed?" The rider indicated the grave.

"No, we just found them. Two dead men and one pretty woman. They were staked out here. Ride around. Escatar will show you the corpses."

The messenger reined his excited horse over there. At the sight of the bodies his face turned white. Obviously he knew them. About to throw up, he raced back for the column.

"Does he know them?" Murty asked, having snuck up behind Slocum and looking around him.

He nodded.

The colonel and two others rode up. "Good day, sir. My name is Colonel Charles Bradford. My man tells me you have the body of my niece and two other men."

"We rode up on them about a half hour ago. They were already dead and badly mutilated. We planned to bury them. They were naked, and there is no sign of anything else around here."

"Bury the men if you will please. I will take my niece's remains to Fort Washington and have her grave closer to me. I am sorry."

"Where is that?"

"Near Camp Supply on Wolf Creek. We are forming a new nation out here. Washington will be its name. The federals have no use for this country. So we will carve a new nation here. And in the remaining time we plan to kill off all these red infidels. A shame that girl is dead. My wife will mourn her passing. I never caught your name, trader?"

"Slocum."

"I see."

No, that dumb stiff shirt didn't see anything. This wild land and his small army would get their asses kicked in by the Plains Indians that abounded out there.

In the morning his own bunch would be swinging southeast to Fort Hayes, where there were some real soldiers, and they'd be delivering their hides to Bart Stowe, the man with his money invested in Slocum's ragtag outfit.

The colonel's men were already heading off. They'd bound the girl's body in a fine expensive wool blanket to carry her back in. Their old one would have done her—she didn't care, that was for damn certain.

He felt Murty bend his knees with hers from behind him. "Let's go eat. I've got it ready."

He spoke in Spanish, "Food's ready!"

They all nodded. Job completed, shovels on their shoulders, they went to eat.

Slocum sat on a wooden bench they got out for him. The men sat cross-legged on the ground. Murty's buffalo steaks had been cooked on a grill; hot biscuits were from a Dutch oven. Then each man had a can of peaches for desert. Murty soon joined Slocum and sat down with her bare knees exposed below the lace hem on her dress.

Nothing like a whore who wanted to show off her body parts. Murty was a nice mess. Hard worker, great cook, and she really liked to make wild love in a bedroll. The Iowa farm girl was no princess; he'd call her chubby, but on a woman emerging from her teens that could be cute too. Her reddish hair was in braids, and her freckled face, most of the time, was smiling. But she was stout as a bull, and could out-shoot or out-cuss most of his men.

How long she'd plied her trade in a house of ill repute, he had no idea. But she'd confronted him at a fort on the north side of the Platte. Told him she was the best cook he could hire and the wildest piece of ass he could find to sleep with. In twenty-four hours he'd found out she was well versed at both and hired her. After three months of being out there, they were headed back for Fort Hayes, Kansas, to meet Bart Stowe and deliver him their stacks of buffalo hides.

Slocum had figured out that at buffalo hunting, he could glance over his shoulder lots less for anyone looking for him and also make some good money to sustain his being on the run. Stowe had been fair dealing with him the last time, so he expected the same this time around. They had enough hides on board that they needed to go back, unload, and restock on food and ammo. The damn stink of their freight was imbedded in his nose. He'd never ever forget it either.

"That old sumbitch really going make a new country out here?" she asked.

"Hell, no. There have been hundreds like him thought they could mutiny against the U.S., and in the end the forces put them down like a boot stomping a mouse in the corner."

"He knew those other dead men, didn't he?"

"I think so. One man had been tattooed in a war prison."

"You know him?"

"No. But I figure he was a soldier of fortune like the rest of Bradford's men."

"Had they run off with that girl?"

"I suspect, if you want the truth, that the colonel was out looking for her."

She ate a piece of buff off her fork and chewed on it. "Makes you wonder, don't it?"

"Oh some. She was pretty enough to run off with."

She grinned and laughed. "You ought to know, you've run off with plenty of them."

"That's how I got you."

"Yeah, but I ain't so good-looking, darling."

"You are to me."

She blushed, waving the long-bladed jackknife at him she used to eat with. "Keep talking, big man. It will give you all the pussy you can stand."

They both laughed.

The next morning, she was up before daylight and had her helper building a fire. She cooked them oatmeal with raisins and brown sugar stirred in, and her secret was the vanilla and almond flavoring she added. Slocum's Mexican crew thought she was a chef he'd hired from some fancy restaurant she was so damn good at feeding the men.

Their axle went squeaking off across the prairie with their stinking treasures, making twenty miles a day by him pushing them and their livestock. His men knew full well there would be plenty of Indian squaw whores to fuck and lots of wildcat whiskey at their destination. So they pushed too.

The line of cottonwoods distinguished the Arkansas

River that trailed out of what would later be Colorado to join the Mississippi in south Arkansas. But its water source across the plains made the way for so many wagon trains that took that route to the Rockies. The leaves had already been frosted and they looked golden in the distance. Fort Hayes was close by.

Slocum saw the mountains of hides and the cooking fire smoke first. The hide piles looked like hills, and the large Conestoga freight wagons were circled around preparing to load them up and take them to places where the skins could be moved onto a river craft, and then at New Orleans they'd be piled onto boats for Germany, where they'd be made into harness leather by an undisclosed formula. That secret had made the hide business a wild success for men like Stowe.

Slocum chose a place for his men to set up camp. When his wagons were circled, he ordered that two sober men must guard the camp night and day. If anything was lost they would have to pay for it out of their pay. When he was told to unload, they all must be there and work or only get half their pay. He issued each man a two-dollar advance and made Escatar the camp boss. They'd also have to do their own cooking, but Philippe, who helped Murty, could do that. Slocum mounted the gray horse, pulled Murty up behind the cantle on his saddle, and nodded good-bye.

She was giggling like usual. "Don't you boys fuck nothing I won't."

They all laughed at her words. Slocum decided they knew more English than he'd thought.

"Where will we go?" she asked, leaning forward and shoving a boob into his back.

"Find a bathhouse and then a hotel room and a good bottle of whiskey. We can celebrate all we want, can't we?"

"Yahoo!" she shouted. "A man of my dreams. You are. You are."

Her arms around his waist, she squeezed him tight from

behind, then kissed his ear. "Goddamn you, Slocum. I don't ever want to lose you."

To be perfectly honest, he didn't want to lose her either. The girl who giggled every time he stuck his dick in her tight cunt. Not once in a while, but every time.

2

Before they took a bath, they stopped at a dress shop and she picked out a new dress. A blue one, and the seamstress was about to blush as she pinned the hem up above Murty's knees and agreed to attach the lace she'd picked out to go on there.

Standing red-faced with excitement, Murty asked Slocum, "Now, won't I look spiffy in this new dress?"

"Spiffy enough for me, Murty."

Outside the dressing blind space, she took off her new dress and began to put on her old one. The poor lady who owned the shop hurried to be sure her door was locked and shade drawn, so no one would be exposed to Murty's uncovered flesh. Slocum tried not to smile as she wiggled into her old dress and shoved it down over her butt.

"We won't be back too soon," she said to the lady; then she took Slocum's arm and they went to find Loo Ling's Bath House. They found it, and the bell rang overhead. A short Chinese man bowed. "Chew want bathie?"

"Yeah, Hop Sing, we both need a bath," Slocum said to him.

"No Hop Sink here. Bath for men only."

"You don't understand. We are both going to take a bath. So get the water ready. How much?"

"Twenty-five cents for you. No let her in." He waved his hands like Murty was out of the deal.

"Here's a dollar for her. Now, get the water hot."

"Bath house for men. No women."

"Now, goddamn it, I offered you a dollar. Four times the price for a man. I am going to get my gun out and shoot you if you don't get your ass to heating water. You understand?"

Loo held up his hands. "No shoot. No shoot. Me get hot water."

"Much better," Slocum said. "Come on, darling. We're getting baths."

She shook her head warily. "Well, God Almighty, what was wrong with that Chinaman anyway?"

"He didn't want any women pissy in his bathtubs."

"Aw, Slocum, he was plum crazy. What woman is going to piss in her bathwater?"

"I don't know, but we are getting two baths."

"Oh, I knew you'd work it out, darling."

"Bath ready," Loo said and bowed.

"Thank you, sir," Slocum said, and they went into the sour-smelling bathing room. It was dimly lighted, and two copper tubs steamed up ready for them. They undressed, and Slocum helped Murty step into hers.

"Woo! It sure is hot," she said, halfway into it and Slocum holding her arm in case she wanted out. "I'll be fine. But it is hot."

With her standing, hugging her melon-size breasts, she soon was laughing. "Maybe he's trying to cook and eat us."

"He might want to eat you, but I'd be gristly enough that he'd throw my meat out to the dogs."

His words had her laughing so hard she stopped edging her butt down into the water. "My lands, this is the hottest water I've ever been in. But boy, does my back feel better. You need me to scrub your back?"

"I can do it with this long-handled brush."

"Oh, I can do that too. Whew, I may just set here for the rest of the day. It feels wonderful."

"I knew you'd like it."

"Oh, I am so damn dumb. I never thanked you for that new dress. I about cried when I saw me in it in the mirror— oh, Gods. And I never thanked you."

"I am thanked enough to have you."

"No, that ain't any excuse. I been in that stinking buff-hide camp for a couple of months. Them boys're sweet. They're good to me. You got me all I need to feed them. And you made me pine every day for nights in your arms. I couldn't've been anywhere else and been any happier."

She threw water at him. "Damn, you big lug. I've been having fun."

"So have I, Murty. Now it's turned cold out, I can get some wool-lined boots made for you while we're here."

"It would beat freezing my toes off. I'd love some."

Slocum came over and poured water on her to rinse her off. She stood on a chair and rinsed him off. Then they dried and re-dressed. Slocum found that the door was locked to get back out. He beat on it.

Loo opened it and bowed. "You get good bath?"

"We sure did. Thank you."

Three whiskered men in dirt-glazed buckskins were standing waiting to get in—to bathe, Slocum guessed. They were ogling Murty and making out-loud comments.

"Hey would ya sell her?" The guy hardly out of his teens was fondling his crotch and grinning big, looking at her like she was for sale.

"Get back, you dumb son of a bitch, or you won't live to see sundown."

"Yeah—"

His words were cut off by the way Slocum drew his gun in unseen speed and faced them with it cocked.

"Hey, hey, we don't mean nothing—" They held their hands out to stop him.

He gave Murty a head toss for her to go on. Then he edged by the men and went out on the boardwalk. In the sunlight he spun the cylinder so the empty chamber would be under the hammer, then holstered it.

"Those men back there—"

"Were animals. This whole trading post is full of men who have forgotten any manners or respect."

She made a short nod. "I savvy that."

He could tell she was shocked by their actions. "Stay close. Let's see if the dress is done."

She gave him a nod like she was on edge, and they went down the boardwalk to the shop. Inside the dress and hat store, the seamstress held the dress up for Murty's approval.

"Oh, it is wonderful. Isn't it, Slocum?"

"Very nice. Now, go behind the Chinese folds and dress back there for her."

"Oh." She agreed and went back there to change.

Slocum chuckled, but the storeowner quietly thanked him. He paid her for the dress while Murty rummaged around behind the screen getting dressed. Singing a bawdy song about some girl looking for a man, she emerged looking bright-eyed.

"It is the best dress I have ever owned. Thank you so much."

He nodded. "I'm ready. You look fine."

"Oh, you'd say that if I was in a gunnysack. He's the best man I ever had," she said to the seamstress. "And I'd swear to it."

They went back to camp. Two men were on guard duty.

Murty slipped off the back of the gray horse and waved at the men, then spun around in her new dress. They whistled and cheered.

"You are *mucho bueno*," one of them shouted.

A second took his horse to be put up.

"Everyone in town?" he asked.

"*Sí.*"

"I hope they are careful. The town is very dangerous."

"Ah, *sí patrón*. Escatar warned all of us before the others left to keep our heads low. Some of the town men might pick on them for being Mexicans."

"If anyone has any trouble, wake me. I will go rescue them if I can."

"We appreciate you, señor. Have a good night."

"Have you eaten?"

The man shrugged.

"She will feed us in a short while."

"I will tell Paco."

Murty fixed them supper and they thanked her. They said they'd do the dishes, so Slocum and Murty went off for a place to spread out his bedroll. He scraped the ground of brush, twigs, and rocks with the side of his boot sole before he spread it out. He sat down, and she pulled off his boots, teasing him some about the day.

"Had you not figured out I wanted to shock that store lady a little by dressing outside them folding deals? I just loved to see her squirm a little." She was chuckling about taking her dress off over her head. "But hey, big man, this is the finest dress I have ever owned."

"It shocked her all right."

"If she has a husband, I bet it embarrasses her to have sex." She was giggling again. "Poor thing."

They were undressed and under the cover of a light blanket. "We unloading tomorrow?" she asked,

"I don't know. I ain't seen him so far, but he's around I bet."

Her hand was playful rolling around his cock and making it rise. Then between her laughing they were kissing hard. He used two fingers on his left hand to check her lubrication. She usually was slick, but if not, it only took him a short while to get enough of her juices going down there by finger fucking her.

"Damn, you are a loving machine," she whispered. "I am so damn spoiled with you. Get on me. I am ready for you to shovel coal into my furnace."

"Hell, Murty, you are always ready for loving." He rose on his knees and laughed, then shifted up between her raised short legs. She spread them wide, and he shoved the nose of his erection inside her, and she oohed out loud.

"Damn, you're like Old Faithful at Yellowstone, spouting off about every half hour."

The next twenty minutes they were lost in each other's rapid response. Swirling around like some great whirlpool, they left the real world for one of passion and hellfire even the Yellowstone geyser could not match. The thin skin on the head of his dick felt stretched at last to the final place. Then two red hot needles struck him in the cheeks of his ass and he came hard. She screamed and then fainted.

Making him stay on top of her, she used her fingers to part the hair on her face. "Oh, damn, that was gut-wrenching chilling. You know I could do that all day with you."

He kissed her wet mouth and took all her breath away, which wasn't hard. His rock-hard, corded belly to her solidly muscled one, they savored their closeness, and he kind of rocked his dick a little in and out of her.

"We better sleep some," she said. "That unloading will be hard work tomorrow. But if you get horny in the night, you wake me up."

"I will." He rose off of her and she dried him off with a towel.

"I bet I smelled better, anyhow?"

"You always smell like a woman. That excites me."

"I'm like a doe deer that's always in heat. That's my problem."

She rolled over with the towel between her legs to staunch the leaking. Her good-size butt against him, he threw his arm over her and squeezed her tit.

"Oh, that felt wonderful." And she giggled then shuddered in pleasure under his arm.

They slept till before dawn. She had a wonderful alarm clock in her head and always had breakfast ready before the sun came up. She was too damn neat and sexy for him to lose, as long as no bounty hunter showed up looking for him. Probably more wanted fugitives hiding out there in the buffalo-hunting business than anywhere else in the country. All of them tough enough that only a damn fool or a grizzly bear would mess with them.

He'd needed to find his man Stowe or his underling and get the hides checked in. When all the skins were off his hands, he'd feel better. At almost five dollars a hide there was real money in the business, and as with gold dollars, the temptation to steal always existed and crime was worse here than it would be in some small farm town in the Midwest.

He was eating her thick oatmeal recipe and sipping strong coffee. Several hungover helpers, moaning and grumbling, came to join them, plus the two guards.

She acted like cheerful Murty, saying, "Oh, you poor babies. Did you drink too much keg-head whiskey last night?"

"Oh, *sí*. Way too much."

"Were them Indian whores pretty last night too?"

"No, not near as pretty as you are."

Then she giggled and spoke to him. "See how lucky you are?"

"I wouldn't stick my dick in any of them even drunk." Slocum shook his head and handed her the bowl for some more.

When she bent over to fill his bowl, the lace of her new dress didn't hardly cover but a small portion of her freckled ass. Nice view from his seat, but she did that for him to see it; otherwise she'd have squatted down.

Everyone fed and given coffee, she sat on the bench beside him, gripped the edge of it with her fingers beside her legs, and rocked on her ass. The sun was beginning to pink the eastern sky. Ravens were gathering to look for scraps, and as the cooler night wind lay down, the hides began filling the air with the rancid smell of green skins. Later in the day, the sun-powered wind would recover and threaten to blow away every flag and hat across Kansas.

Slocum went to look for Stowe. He finally found him playing cards in the Oxbow Saloon. A big man smoking a large cigar that he kept clamped in his teeth. He wore a trail-dusted suit coat and even a string tie. The white shirt was food-stained, and all of it must have been tailor-made, because they didn't make store-bought that large.

"Ah, Slocum. I heard you was coming in. How many hides?"

"Seven hundred."

"Holy shit. You've been killing the fire out of them." He looked over his hand and spoke to the dealer. "Give me two cards." Then he tossed his two discards onto the table.

The man under the visor dealt him two more.

"Goddamn, that was all right. Two aces the same suit."

His fellow players jerked awake around the table. "What was that?"

"Just kidding. Hell, you can't take a joke?"

"Not when you've been beating the hell out of us."

"I finish this hand, Slocum'll set in for me. I've got to go empty my bowels."

"I may lose your money."

"Naw, it's a lucky seat, been in it a long time."

"You still got Murty?" one guy asked him.

"Still got her. No one else wants her."

"He's lying. He has the sweetest freckle-assed woman on the prairie."

"I seen her on the Platte," a gray-headed old fart said, betting two dollars. "She's head and shoulders over any woman around here. Except that niece of Colonel Bradford's up at Camp Supply. Wow, she's a real looker."

Slocum took Stowe's seat. "She's dead. We found her and two men scalped, mutilated, and staked out on the prairie seven days northwest of here."

"Ah, the hell you say. Any idea who did it?"

Slocum shook his head and looked at his new cards. He had two fours and an ace to keep. The raise was two bucks. He tossed his in and took two cards. Things went well, and he drew another four and an ace for a full house. The next raise was three dollars; he raised it to five, and a bearded teamster raised it five more. There were two players left to decide. One of them raised it five more, and the other tossed his cards in. Someone called. "I got three queens."

The next man said he had three jacks and shook his head, tossing in his cards

The three-queen player was grinning like a possum eating shit when he looked over at Slocum. "What have you got?"

"A full house fours and aces."

The expectant winner slumped in his chair. "I'll be a sumbitch. I had the best hand of the night and you beat me. Go tell Stowe to get off the pot. You're luckier than he is."

Everyone laughed.

"Say, Slocum, you figure out who killed her?" an older man asked.

"No. They were stripped naked and not one small item was around them. Besides her, one of the men about thirty had prisoner-of-war numbers tattooed on his right arm."

"Giles Gifford."

"You knew him?"

"Hell, yes. He was a captain in the Mississippi Cavalry."

"Well him and a dark-haired man was the other one. I figured they'd all been with Bradford and she ran off with them."

"Or they kidnapped and took her."

"I don't know," Slocum said. "Bradford took her body back to bury her at his Camp something."

"Washington," the man said. "He has big plans to build a nation out here."

"Hell, folks been planning those sort of things since they shot Alexander Hamilton," another man said. "They never get nowhere. What made you think they kidnapped her?"

"I don't think she'd left there with Gifford."

"Why not?"

"To be honest," the old man said and picked up his new hand. "He was a real prick. No one liked him. He was mad all the time. Like he was still in prison. I doubt she'd even given him the time of day. There wasn't a black guy killed there too?"

"No. Why?"

"He had an ex-slave that grew up with him and still waited on him hand and foot. Some guys would tell him Lincoln set him free, and he'd say 'Not me. My momma said long as I lived I was responsible for him and his safety. Lincoln don't make no never mind for me.'"

"What was his name?"

"Joshua Gifford. I figured that Gifford's father was one

that sowed his seeds in his black mother, and that was why she did that."

"He wasn't staked out there on the plains."

"You ever see him, you won't miss him. He stands way over six feet tall, broad-backed and powerful as any bull."

That was a new twist to the murders Slocum had found out there. There was or had been a black man in the deal somewhere. Hell only knew the story, and them dead folks weren't telling anyone.

He played three more hands and won the third one. Stowe came back to watch him rake in the pot.

"We better sell them hides in the morning to Crawford and Hull's yard. Start unloading at seven o'clock in the morning."

"We will be there."

"I can settle up with you and your men the next day. You are going back, aren't you?"

"Yeah, but it will be damn cold by then. Need to cut lots of firewood, which cuts down on our killing time."

"I know that. But I think hides will go to ten dollars by spring."

"Why's that?"

"Just a feeling. Them Germans ain't got no buffalo to run down over there. Hides are getting harder to find. Take along some more men to cut your firewood. We can afford them."

Slocum nodded. "Good. I'll start looking for four more men to cut the firewood that we will need and to be camp helpers."

"You did well this time. I hope you can get that many more of them hides."

"We'll try our damndest."

"Hey, I know I am lucky to have you in charge. I have three outfits out there. You beat them by fifty percent, and they try hard."

"You heard about that killing?"

"I did. Sounded bad."

"I think these Plains Indians are really going to explode one of these days. They ever join hands and do it as one, there won't be a buffalo hunter left alive between here and the Rockies."

Stowe nodded like he fully understood Slocum's concern.

"We will see what happens."

"Be careful. I need you."

"As I said, I'll go look for some more help today."

"My man Cayman will be at the unloading."

"Good. He can argue with his grader about the hides."

"He knows how. I better get going. You be careful. This camp is real hell. Two or three guys die every weekend, and more during the week."

"I agree."

Slocum went back to camp and checked on Murty. He swung her up behind him on the gray horse. They rode down to the river to see about some men he could hire to cut firewood. There were several Mexicans down there who'd come to find work. They lived in shack towns where the Indian whores camped and where some other breeds loafed around like buzzards and slept all the time.

Slocum spoke in Spanish to several young men who were looking for work.

"Where did you live before you came here?" he asked a young man who looked smarter than the others.

"Taos."

"My name is Slocum."

"Mine is Diego."

"Why did you come here?"

"To work, señor. They said there were many jobs here."

"Maybe they lied to you."

He smiled. "*Sí*, maybe so."

"Have you ever worked for the Comancheros?"

"Oh, *sí*."

"Can you shoot a rifle?"

"Oh, *sí*."

"This is very dangerous out there."

He nodded. "I know, we were attacked coming up here."

"What did you do?"

"I shot a cap-and-ball rifle at them."

"We have Winchesters. You ever shot one?"

"No, señor."

"I can teach you how to do that. You will have to cut firewood and bring it to camp so we don't freeze this winter."

"I can do that."

"Can you find three more men who will work at doing that? If they don't work, you will have to do it all."

"I can find three good men."

"I pay fifty cents a day and food. You do good work, I will get you a bonus."

He nodded. "When do we start?"

"My camp is north of the fort. Ask for Slocum. Bring all your clothes, 'cause it will be cold. You don't have warm clothes, I will advance you money to buy some."

"Can we come today?"

"Yes. My cook will have supper in late afternoon."

"We will be there."

"See you there, Diego."

He shook the man's hand and went back to where Murty was standing with the horse.

"He the new man?" she asked

"His name is Diego. He is getting three more to cut wood for us."

"Nice-looking boy, isn't he?" She was watching Diego celebrate some with his friends over their good luck.

"He looked smart enough to do the job. He has been with the Comancheros. So he should be camp- wise. He'd never shot a Winchester, but had shot cap-and-ball weapons."

"Good. We will have more men in camp to help defend us."

"Yes, we will. Once we hit the bad weather, those Indians won't have the pony power to raid our camp. But killing buffalo will be harder too. We will take grain for our animals so we have them to use. Stowe knows these winter hunts are expensive, but he thinks hides will be ten dollars next spring, so he wants us to try to get as many as we can."

"I would like to be where it is warm. Where is that?"

"San Antonio."

"It never gets cold down there in winter?" she asked.

"Very seldom."

"What can we do down there to make money?"

"I don't know or I'd be down there."

"Make lots of money so we can go live there the next winter."

He mounted and swung her up to go back to camp. "I will try."

"We get the hides unloaded tomorrow and we'll have more help, huh?"

"Yes." He clapped her leg beside his and they short loped to camp.

The men were rounded up and in camp for supper. The new crew members came and were introduced. They filed through the chow line and smiled, raising their plates to Murty and saying, "*Gracias, señora.*"

She just smiled. "They are eager-acting boys."

"They also came to eat tonight, I bet, because they had little to eat down there."

"What did they eat?"

"Ask them. I have no idea. I need to be sure they have clothes enough."

"They will be better off with us, won't they?"

"I hope so. And four more guns if they can shoot them. We'll have target practice this week before we go out."

"How far did they come to get up here?"

"Hundreds of miles, I would say, but they probably had no idea except someone said there was work up here. Diego said they fought Indians coming up here with that cap-and-ball rifle. I'll get some Winchesters and ammo for them tomorrow."

"I'm ready to go to bed. Are you? Be a long day unloading tomorrow."

They went to their bedroll, had a quick roll in the hay, and slept till before dawn. She woke him and quickly put on her old dress for the day's work.

Animals were harnessed and one man chosen to guard the camp and the supply wagons. They ate Murty's oatmeal and drove over to the Crawford and Hull hide yard.

A big Portuguese named Cayman, who worked for Stowe, met them. The buyers were two white men and still looked half-drunk as they staggered down to meet the sellers. They wanted two new piles, and they had to look at each robe to be sure it had no holes cut in it by the skinner. Whole hides were the most valuable. Others were going to be discounted. So Slocum made his men set aside any damaged hides to argue over later. He also had a man with a pencil and a cedar slab for a board to write on and to count with each of the buyers. His man used the five-count system of tally marks—four marks and then one slash across them for the fifth.

They had arguments with the buyers over the condition of some of the hides. Cayman had one hide buyer, Slocum the other, and the deal went on for hours, until every wagon and cart was empty. The sun had warmed the air a lot and the wind was out of the south.

They were down to ten hides to argue over. Weary of the bickering, Slocum stepped in. "Take them or we load up the rest. My men can reload them."

"All right," the buyer with the billy-goat beard said. "We'll take them too."

"How many hides do you have down?" Slocum asked them.

"We've got to count."

Murty had handed him a paper that said, "706." She'd already added both lists up, and she was good at math.

"Six ninety-two," the yard man said.

"Count them again. You are fourteen short. Want to restack them?"

"No." He wrote Slocum's number on his report, and the Portuguese signed it for Stowe. He shook hands with Slocum. "I like you. Every time you sell your hides you have the numbers right."

"Tell Stowe we will be ready for him to pay us in the morning."

"He'll be there."

3

From the yard, Slocum went to Vanwinkle's Trading Post and bought four used Winchesters. He was well versed on how to examine them. The rifles' breeches were made of brass and wore out fast; well-used ones were worthless. These guns were all right, in almost new condition, and he took them back to camp. Before he left, he'd told the boys to get two gunnysacks of old bottles together and they'd have target practice for everyone when he got back, and if their rifles were not clean, he said, they should clean them. Each man's weapon would be tested. If he couldn't shoot it, he might be fired. Slocum's rules having been set down, he expected the men would be ready for their rifle practice when he returned.

Escatar had shown the new boys how to use a Winchester, so when Slocum issued them their new rifles, they were ready. Belly down, they each had a shot at the bottles.

"I will have to etch your name on the receiver today," Slocum said. "You lose yours, you pay for it. You steal another man's gun, I will shoot you with it. When we get through, clean them. You don't do a good job cleaning it each time, the rifle will jam, and that endangers all of us. So don't let that happen. You shoot a man for no good reason, we will hang you. If you fight with another man working for me, you can walk home unarmed."

The new men shot well and acted pleased to have their weapons. Escatar made them shoot again and again, one at a time. All but one man busted the bottles. He said he could not see them. Slocum remembered him and decided that he must need glasses, but he worked hard, so Slocum excused him. The man thanked him gratefully.

They ate Murty's lunch, then sat around and cleaned their rifles. It still stunk like hides around the place to Slocum, who etched the names of the new men on their guns. When Stowe came to pay them, he had two men armed with Greener shotguns. Cayman was one of them. Stowe introduced Slocum to the other man, named Holt.

They paid every man fifty dollars, and the men repaid Slocum his two-dollar advance. Then Stowe thanked the men in Spanish. That over, Slocum issued the order that two men must stay sober and guard the camp. Meanwhile his boss paid Murty one hundred and fifty for her three months. Then he paid Slocum three hundred.

"I appreciate all you do," Stowe said, seated behind the table with Slocum beside him. "I can buy some two-pint crock jugs of firewater. Could you trade it to the Indians out there for hides? They cost me a dollar and a half apiece. If we can trade 'em for a good buff hide, I could make some real money."

Slocum nodded.

"The deal is the U.S. marshal could fine us all if we get caught. This stuff has no tax stamp on it. What do you think?"

"Hide it under some trade blankets. What do the jugs cost?"

"Three dollars. Your idea is a good one. You've been swapping blankets for hides too, huh?"

"Yeah. You know drunk Indians can be tough customers to deal with."

"Oh yeah. I'll cut you in for fifty cents apiece on both of the jugs."

"Sounds good. How bad is that stuff?"

"Horse piss, but it will make them drunk."

"Of course they will want to taste it. So we will use some for that purpose."

"No problem. We can load it in the bed of one of your wagons, cover it with grain sacks for our animals, and then trade blankets. Those small crocks are harder to bust than glass. But in case of a wreck, we could lose them all." Stowe shrugged.

"Now I'm a whiskey trader. Oh well, maybe we can make money with it all."

"Hey, you got Murty. That is the cutest redhead in the whole country of Kansas. Man, when I saw her today in that new dress, I said, that sumbitch Slocum screws with her every night—whew."

Slocum agreed with a nod. "Hell, you can trade some of your whiskey for some young squaw who hasn't got the clap. She'd keep you entertained."

Stowe nodded. "I should do that. You find me one, I'll pay you for her."

"I'll see." *Trade for your own* was his unspoken answer. "We will leave in about four days. I want to shoe some of the horses. Some don't need it."

"Day after tomorrow, I'll send a farrier out here who has a forge setup and blower. And you be careful. Send the wagon you aim to carry the whiskey and goods in with about four men to help load it."

"I'll send the best driver too."

Stowe laughed. "Do that. Good luck. Keep your head down."

They parted. Stowe went and found Escatar, the broad-shouldered man who served as his foreman. He had been a seaman in his younger days and knew every trick in fist fighting and knives, and bore the scars to prove it. He smiled a lot while buffalo hunting—claimed it was so much better than being at sea. Slocum didn't know much about the sea except for some coastal sailing in the Gulf to get from New Orleans to Texas ports.

Slocum and Escatar stood off to the side. "We have a new problem we don't need to talk about out loud where the others can hear. Stowe wants to trade some whiskey for hides with the Indians. Keeping the men out of that supply will be hard. It is sorry whiskey, untaxed. If the federal agents find it, we will be fined. So it will be a new source of trouble, huh?"

Muscled arms folded over his chest, his man shook his head under the knit cap. "I will explain a hands-off policy."

"Good. Farrier is coming tomorrow to shoe the horses that need shoes. We will load the wagon I spoke about tomorrow too."

"I will take it in to his warehouse."

"Yes. You will need four men to load it."

"No problem."

"I think we can have our supplies loaded and be back out on the plains in four days."

"Those were four good men you hired. They will work."

"I thought so. Existing down there in that river camp taught them a job is good fortune."

"Her cooking too."

Slocum agreed.

He went to town and played cards that night in the rowdy Oxbow Saloon. Stowe wasn't there. Lots of gossip was passed around about the Indians and their uprisings. His gambling luck held, and he won enough to break even. When he started out of the batwing doors into the night, he heard a shot. Then, in the dark street, he saw the figure of the man who had made the shot from his horse. Slocum's gun drawn, he aimed it at the shooter and shot the one threatening everyone. Hard-hit in the chest, his gun went off harmlessly into the air and he pitched off the horse and down on his face in the dirt.

Customers rushed outside to join those on the street. Slocum was kneeling down by the man the shooter had fired at.

"You all right?"

"No. I'm gonna die. He got me." The man strained against the pain.

"What was this about?"

"Spanish treasure. Get the map out of my saddlebags. There's a fortune out there."

"Where is your horse?"

"The bay under the Mexican saddle."

A glance up, and Slocum saw the wooden saddle horn shining in the light from the saloon. "What is your name?"

"John Trent—" Slocum knew at that point that the man would soon die.

"You know this guy that you shot?" one man called, standing over by the shooter.

Slocum shook his head.

"He's Miles Hampton. Missouri congressman Horace Hampton's son."

"What the hell was he shooting John Trent for?" He let the crowd think he knew Trent. He'd planned to get the man's horse and map and then bury him.

No one had an answer. There was no sign of any law showing up. They helped Slocum load Trent's corpse on his horse. He mounted the gray and took the lead. The other dead man's body was being loaded up by a funeral man in a black suit, who put him into a hearse. No doubt the under-taker expected to get paid by the father.

Once Slocum was back in camp, Escatar came to see about the body over the horse. Others joined him to help. Murty brought a candle lamp for them to see by.

Escatar sent the men for shovels. Slocum found the map and stuck it inside his shirt. He also found several letters, which he retrieved. Escatar went through the rest of Trent's pockets, taking his money and personal things out. There was not much. His clothing was threadbare like most men's on the frontier. His boots needed repair, but they and the rest of his wardrobe were handed out to the men who needed them, and Trent was buried in his underwear.

At a table with only Murty and his Escatar, Slocum spread out the map. In the lamplight he could see the care the mapmaker had taken with a pen. A compass drawing showed the direction at the top of the map to be north.

"What does it show?"

"Where some Spanish treasure was buried according to the dead man. He gave it to me."

"Where is this at?" Murty asked.

"Western Kansas. I would say along the Arkansas."

"Tell me, why would they have lots of gold or whatever way the hell out there?" Murty shook her head in disgust and disbelief.

"Good question. But the treasure has been a rumor for years. They said it was hidden by a column of Mexican sol-diers who were guarding the treasure when they were attacked by Indians. They buried the treasure so no one could find it. One boy snuck away in the fury of the battle, and it took him over a year to make his way home."

"Did the boy come back to find it?"

"The say he did, but he was unsure where exactly it was buried, and they dug many places and never found any-thing."

"So how did this dead man tonight find it?" Murty asked, still not sounding convinced it was all real.

"Hell, I don't know. But that son of a bitch shot him for a real reason. He too may have had a map to lead him there and maybe didn't want Trent to find the treasure first. Or else he hoped to get the map off Trent after he was dead."

"So then two parties will be going to look for it? Us and the rest of the gang from the man you shot?"

"I don't know about the man I shot. I figure the congressman's son's bunch might give up now that he's dead. They probably needed his daddy's money to outfit such an expedition."

"Can we go out there and look for it and still kill buffalo?" Murty asked.

"Sure. It is right out there where they graze."

"Good, let's find it so I can go live in a fancy two-story house somewhere and have tea with people."

"You'd be bored to death, Murty."

"I am bored to death now every night. But I love it." Then she laughed at her own joke.

4

They left Fort Hayes an hour before the sun rose. A nip in the air, harness jingled and leather squeaked as the draft animals hit their collars and strained to move the loaded wagons. A few had little to haul, but they were hitched to younger horses who needed more training. Half were mule teams that brayed a lot. Slocum wished they were all mules, but besides being more expensive they were hard to find. And most that were for sale would kick a man's head off, and he didn't need to tend to anyone kicked in the head—usually they never got their right mind back and posed a real problem for those tasked with caring for them.

In those things in Trent's saddlebags, Slocum had read the letters from his wife, who lived with her parents on a farm in western Iowa. In her letters, she had been concerned about his health out there, and the dangers he faced. She wanted him to come back home to farm and stop his treasure hunting so they could have family and a life together. One letter, Slocum recalled, addressed her concern about Trent dealing with the congressman's son. She had doubts about anything to do with that man. Trent should have listened to her.

Slocum sent her a note telling her that her husband was dead and had no things of value that Slocum could send on to her.

A week later they set up on the bend in the Arkansas that was marked on the map. Slocum began to search the area with Murty riding on the back of his horse. One day riding close to the river he spotted a rusted old Spanish spur imbedded in the sand. He let Murty down and then dismounted to recover the once very ornate spur. It was corroded by rust and grime, so he found a rag and they polished the spur with sand and water.

"Well at least we found their spur, huh?" She giggled and shook her head. "Way off up here, I bet that they were horny bastards when those Indians killed them."

"This happened way before wagons even used this route. Maybe over a hundred years ago."

She looked around and across the shallow river. "But where did they bury their treasure, huh?"

Big question. He had only one answer. "Have you ever witched for water in your life?"

"No. But I've seen it done back in Iowa. Why are you asking me that?"

"I don't have any power with a peach branch in my hands, but if you do, we might find it?"

"How do you figure that? You don't need water."

"I was at a party in Biloxi once before the war, and a woman took a peach-branch fork and found a lost ring with it."

Murty scowled at his words. "Aw, I don't believe that could happen."

"You don't know what you have not tried."

"Who has a peach-tree fork out here?"

He pointed at his chest. "I do."

"Where you get that at?"

"People have thrown out pits all along this trail for years, and two days ago I cut a few along the river that had sprouted up. "Want to try one?"

"Sure, but it won't do nothing for me."

"Wait and see."

"You think they buried them right here?"

"Hell, darling, I wasn't here. But we found a spur here and we may find a treasure here."

"Okay, get the branch."

"Coming right up."

She shook her head at him like she thought he was crazy. Then she giggled. "I don't know about you at times, big man. You can come up with some real strange ideas." Rambling on about how she didn't believe there was any magic in a peach tree—she waited.

When he returned, she held the small fork in her hands out in front of her and began to stride across the sand in the new wool-lined boots he'd had made for her. Out of nowhere she screamed and dropped the stick like it was on fire. Then she started backing up like she'd seen the devil himself or a rattlesnake, until she bumped into him and he caught her.

"What in the hell is wrong, woman?"

She hugged him tight. "Oh, my God, that damn stick turned in my hand and then I saw a strongbox down there." Her whole body was trembling as she clung to him and pointed in the direction she had backed away from.

"I've been in spooky deals—b-but never this weird."

"Well the thing is now we need a shovel."

She was still having spasms of chill-like symptoms. "I'm too shaky to try and ride a horse. I'll sit down here while you go get a shovel. I'll be right here waiting."

He charged off on the gray, grabbed a shovel from the camp, and rode back to her in a hurry. When he got back, she was still seated hugging her arms and acting like she was freezing. The sun was too hot for that reaction.

On her feet she ran to him and stood shaking her head in dismay. "Where do you think I got that power?"

"You always had it. The peach fork brought it out in you."

"I damn sure ain't telling anyone but you about it. They'd lock me up if my story was exposed."

He dug for an hour in the soft sand. She began to speak discouragingly about the whole deal. "It probably was all a fluke. Nothing down there, is there?"

Then his shovel struck something hollow.

She jumped up. "What is it? What is it?"

He was standing in the hole tossing the sandy material up on the ground beside her in a large pile. At last he unearthed a metal-bound chest. The dryness out there had preserved the wood from rot. A large lock swung on the hasp when he put the heavy box on the ground and climbed out.

"Oh my God." Her hands pressed to her face, she stood shaking all over. "Looks just like I saw it brand-new."

Kneeling beside it, he used his pistol butt to bust the lock open. She joined him, mumbling about everything at once. The lid was stuck, but he finally pried it open, and the tarnished multiple-sided coins appeared.

"They ain't worth nothing. No one in their right mind would take one of those old things. Shoot, we did all this work for a box full of goddamn junk."

He took out his rag and polished one of the coins in his fingers until a golden hue shone in the sunlight. He heard her suck in her breath.

"Aw sweet Jesus, they are sure enough real gold coins. Holy Christmas, we are rich. You crazy galoot, you found us a fortune." She was hugging and kissing him like a wild woman. "Oh, I am going crazy. I can't wait to get you in bed tonight. I'm going to really take you to the end."

He was covering the hole as fast as he could. "Go cut some sagebrush with my bowie knife. This needs to look like I never disturbed it."

"Right, we have to conceal all this, don't we?"

"Right." His back muscles were beginning to ache from all the heavy digging.

"Where will we hide it?"

"In the false wagon bed under the floor in your wagon."

"Good, you show me. It will be safe there. Now tell me why was all this money way out here in the first place."

"Before Thomas Jefferson bought this land, the Spaniards owned it. They may have been taking all of this to what is now St. Louis. The French got the land back, but Napoleon sold it to finance his wars."

"You think there is more here?"

"Yes."

"Do you think I could find it?"

"Yes."

"That really scares me worse than having bad dreams."

"We need to be careful. There is enough here to be the target of a mutiny of men or a robbery."

"How will we get it back?"

"We can sneak back to camp while all the men are gone hunting. I've heard several shots, so they have work out there. Meanwhile we will hide it."

"Good. You are so wonderful." She hugged his neck and kissed him.

He recovered the peach fork, then led the horse. Seated behind the cantle, she held the heavy box ahead of her on the saddle. They made it back undiscovered and hid the heavy loot in her wagon. He planned to bury the empty box later somewhere else. That would have to do for the time, but there were all sorts of things that bothered him about the safety of their treasure.

Did anyone else come with Trent out there to Fort Hayes? No mention of it in his wife's letters, but did the congressman's son have a search party? As far as Slocum knew, no one had shown up to claim Hampton's body and handle the funeral. He understood that the funeral man had sent a bill to Miles's father in D.C. for his burial costs.

A highly placed congressman like that could sic the U.S. marshals or Pinkerton men on Slocum, to find and arrest him on murder charges. One more damn good reason for him to keep his head down. He'd better back get to killing buffalo. It soon would be too cold and wintry to do much. He also needed to go see about trading some of the newly arrived whiskey for hides.

There were usually some squaws who would come to trade for food when they learned of any camps around close. Though there'd been none so far, one day they'd show up. Slocum could trade for some wolf pelts in full winter fur that would sell well. Also mink and ermine furs, along with the fierce badger skins. It all depended how many tribes were this far west. He knew many tribesmen were down on the Canadian River because winters were a little milder down there and that meant more buffalo, but the area bordered on the Comanche range, and they were too deadly for Slocum to risk being around.

Hunting went well until the first big snow drifted in. Then they fed their animals grain sparingly until they could paw for grass under the snow cover. It was weeks before they could go back for more treasure hunting. From a wandering trader, Slocum bought a pack mule to carry the loot back home.

But before the snow really set in, Murty had covered lots of the riverbed ground with a peach branch, to find only old flint musket works and barrels, the stocks long rotted away, spurs, and some steel spear heads—but no more boxes in that area.

Five Indian women came to trade furs for food at their camp one afternoon. Slocum issued them one bottle of whiskey and told them in sign language that they would owe him three buffalo hides for it. They nodded.

Two days later they came back with six horses and their travois loaded down with buffalo hides and furs to trade for more food and whiskey. At that price Stowe would show a real good profit from his winter work. Diego was off with his three men cutting down trees on an island, for firewood. With the hard freeze on the river, they hoped to get the wood out and back to camp, where the supply was getting low. They each carried a rifle, and Slocum had told them to be alert at all times.

They returned that evening and told him that they had a good stockpile cut up and thought the ice was thick enough to hold up horses and a wagonload of firewood to bring it closer to camp. The ice was eight inches thick where they drew water for the animals and themselves from the river.

Hunting was slowed down by the weather, but more squaws, from different tribes, came to trade for—"with-ski." That was how they pronounced it. One squaw, he knew, had gone away and then slipped back at night to treat some of Slocum's men on her back under the covers for something in trade, maybe for some blankets. There was no trouble; Slocum was amused that life went on as usual even out on the frozen prairie, miles from civilization. He had the lovely Murty to giggle with him in his bedroll at night anyway.

Then a thaw came in February. In the South, where he was raised, they called it oat planting time. He and Murty went back and tried a new place to search for more treasure. They recovered two more treasure chests that day and secured the coins in her wagon. Then he hauled off the empty chests and destroyed them so no one would recognize them.

So far he felt their treasure recovery was going well. There was no telling the value their find amounted to, but the haul was much larger than he'd ever imagined. More squaws came to trade, but he could see that their horses were poor from eating only willows. It was the Indians Achilles heel in the north country. Their horses, in a bad winter, almost starved. Some did, and the ones that survived had to have six weeks of grass to even recover. The southern tribes, like the Comanche, didn't have that handicap, with open grasslands for their horses to graze all winter.

One snowy day, an entire tribe came and pitched camp nearby. It was snowing slantways, and the north wind was cutting through hard. Slocum told everyone to stay with his gun. They had a stout sidewall tent for their meals, and two stoves.

A chief came and talked peace and how he wanted to trade more hides for whiskey. The tent soon was full of tribesmen, women, and children, plus Slocum's men.

Murty went to cooking on top of the metal stove all the buffalo meat she had on hand.

Some of the men ran outside and took an axe to a frozen carcass that they'd dragged in to get her more meat. Soon some of the Indian women began to help her.

She showed them how to pound thawed meat slices tender with her special hammer, then flour them and fry them in boiling lard. The results, passed around to the men, made even the Indians grin. She also made bear tracks in another fry pan of hot melted lard. Cooled some, she broke them in half and fed them to the delighted children. It took two hours to fill everyone. The Indians went back to their tepees when the women got them set up. Slocum never knew how they did it in the howling wind, but he knew from experience that Indian women were as strong as most men.

Escatar spoke to him when the Indians had left, about how many guards should be posted.

"Three? What do you think? They act friendly, but that can change like the wind."

Slocum's man agreed. "Where will you sleep?"

"In her wagon, if you need me."

He nodded. "They were damn sure hungry for her fried meat."

"It was a treat, like the bear tracks."

"Yes. But it will be a long night."

Slocum agreed. He and "Giggly" were soon in their cocoon of blankets to get ready to sleep.

"I am so damn tired from cooking and cooking I don't think I could do much for you."

"Sleep. You did extra well. I can wait."

"Good." She snuggled over on her side with her butt to him, and he curled around her. The first time in nine months they had missed having sex. Whenever they would get into bed, she was ready and nothing stopped them, cycle or whatever. But he had to agree he wouldn't miss it this night with all those Indians so close around them and him thinking about all the danger they might pose, even though there were women and children with them. He slept on edge that night.

Before they left the next day, the Indians had traded thirty hides for ten jugs of whiskey. Stowe's plan worked well. They had also traded hides and other furs for many blankets. Whatever they did with the whiskey was their business, but it would be a hell of a drunk.

The weather let up, and Slocum and his men went back to shooting buffalo. He felt good about their results, and the trading had gone even better than he'd expected, the wood-cutters had brought in a new supply that was stacked high— things were going too good to suit him. He wanted his witch back out there on her peach stick. But the frost, even in the sandy ground, had the Spaniards' gold locked up. He felt there might be as many as two more boxes. The Spaniards must have hid the treasure in various locations so that if treasure hunters found one, the others would still be concealed. Plus the boy who supposedly escaped the massacre and came back years later said, according to rumor, that he could not find any of the chests. But no total on the number was ever spoken.

There was now a large fortune in the false bed of her wagon. But it was a long way from being counted as a windfall. Spring came slow, and the two tried two more discovery trips, with no luck. Supplies were low enough that Slocum decided they needed to head back, so he rounded up the men and told them, "Tomorrow we start back. Feed the horses and mules double rations. We need them strong."

"How many hides?"

"Over six hundred. It was a good hunt." That did not count the ones traded for and all the other kinds of furs they also took in. They were able to move quickly and were back in Fort Hayes in two weeks.

The men drew their two dollars and left for town, leaving two on guard at the camp. Slocum found the banker at home that night and talked to him about the treasure. Aaron Tate was a man in his forties, clear-eyed, with a soft voice. "You have my word. Completely confidential business. What is it?"

"Spanish gold coins."

"A few?"

"No, quite a few. They are over a hundred years old."

"Oh, that is interesting. I suggest you ship them via an insured carrier to St. Louis. We can get a bid there on their value based on the quality."

"I have a woman who will have the power to collect all the money if I am not available. I trust her with my life."

"Then she will also need to sign the agreement."

"She can sign her name and she can count."

"When will you bring the treasure in?"

"Tomorrow."

"She can sign it with you then."

"Fine. I will arrive there when you open."

"I will have some extra security so we can get it into the vault."

Slocum went back and explained the details to Murty. "You will sign and be a partner with me. But if anything happens to me, this money is all yours. Spend it wisely."

She looked solemn. "I don't want anything to happen to you."

"Neither do I, but you may be in charge."

He rounded up Escatar and four other men who were sober and tough. They were set to guard the wagon on the way to the bank and during the unloading the next morning.

Slocum and Murty sacked the coins that night and had it all ready. In the morning she drove the team, and he rode the gray horse with the Winchester across his leg. The men rode inside her wagon with their arms ready.

She halted the wagon at the bank and set the brake at the front door. The guards jumped down, and the treasure was soon shuffled inside. Slocum's men went outside to wait for him. The coins were being counted, and Slocum asked for ten of them in a money sack.

The bank teller took care of that and handed him the sack. He handed it to Murty. "We'll give those to Stowe."

In quick agreement she smiled and nodded. "He deserves them."

The final count came to three thousand and twenty coins.

Tate said, "I am not on top of this market. But I would say about sixty thousand dollars."

She whistled and then she giggled. "Nice job, big man."

He hugged her shoulders. "Let's go eat some breakfast. I'm starved."

5

Emerging through the front door of the bank, Slocum blinked in disbelief at the three men in suits and badges seated on their horses. The man with the drooping mustache asked, "Are you John Slocum?"

"Yes."

"I have a warrant for your arrest for treason and the murder of an agent of the United States, Miles Hampton."

"Don't fight them," Slocum said to his men, who had taken defensive positions. "There is no need for anyone to be killed here. I surrender."

"Tell me, Marshal, what was this Hampton doing for the government when he shot down John Trent in cold blood?"

"According to my papers he was a federal agent investigating the organization trying to form the government of Washington."

The other two deputies took Slocum's gun and bowie knife and put him in handcuffs. He nodded to Murty that it would be all right.

"Take care of my horse," he said to her as they marched him down the boardwalk, he guessed to house him in the fort jail. The deputies looked around a lot, making sure no one was going to break him loose. The marshal led their horses, and he too craned his neck around a lot.

They put him in a cell and acted relieved when he was uncuffed and they were outside the cell door locked by the guard. He asked the jailer if he could have some food, because he had not eaten any since the night before. The man acted stoic and said he would see. That meant nothing,

Nothing came either. Stowe showed up with two good trade blankets, and they searched the blankets and him too before letting him in see Slocum. With an armed guard watching them, they let Stowe talk to Slocum from outside the cell.

"Thanks. This place is not overheated." Slocum used one of the blankets to get under for a coat.

"No problem. I figured it was cold in here. Your damn bond is set at twenty thousand dollars. What in hell did you do?"

"That congressman's boy shot a man named Trent in front of the Oxbow that first night I got back to town. I shot him before he shot me—self-defense. The stuff about me helping that Washington business is bullshit. That's that colonel who thinks he will rebel against the U.S. government up at Fort Supply."

"A good lawyer is coming from Wichita. He will be here in three or four more days. Thanks for those Spanish coins Murty gave me. I'd never seen one of them before in my life. You and Freckles had some luck, huh?"

"We might have found it all."

"I'd heard about that deal for twenty years. I doubted it was even out there."

"It was there but not in one place. They didn't aim for you to find it easy, and I still don't understand their plan to hide it."

"How much did you have to dig up?"

"Oh, fifty acres." Slocum shook his head and smiled. "No, not true—we got lucky is all."

"Well, we'll work to get this sorted out. Freckles is handling the count tomorrow at the yard. She's real business-like. And she knows what is going on—she's is damn upset they arrested you."

"Tell Murty not to worry."

"I will. Sorry—I tried to bail you out, but that twenty thousand is just too steep. We will get it straightened out somehow."

"Thanks, Stowe. Look out for her for me."

"I can do that."

Stowe left him. They brought his food at last: stale bread, some watery cold soup with a few chopped potatoes in it, and something they called coffee. He figured the fare would get no better. Being sent to a military prison meant either that they wanted to impress upon you the importance of not getting thrown back in or that they had no use for you because of the crime you had committed.

He slept most of the night thanks to Stowe's blankets. Lots of moaning and screaming went on—they kept the soldiers that went nuts in there too.

The next day, they emptied his slop bucket and took him in irons before a federal magistrate. Some clerk read the charges against him and they swore him in.

"How do you plead?"

"Not guilty on both counts. I have a lawyer coming, Your Honor."

"He may come here too late. You are to be transferred to the federal court at Leavenworth, Kansas, for your trial shortly."

"Your Honor. There are several witnesses to this man's death that are here locally who will make true statements about my shooting Miles Hampton in self-defense. How will I prove that over there?"

"I can have a clerk take their testimony. However, at present you have no legal representative here."

"Can you hear them, sir?"

"I will consider your request."

"That lawyer is coming as quick as possible."

"The federal prosecuting attorney had requested your immediate transfer to Leavenworth Prison."

"Your Honor, if these men's testimony show you cause that I am innocent, then will you delay my being moved until that is taken?"

"You have forty-eight hours to get them to testify. I will begin to accept them after lunch."

"May I send a message to my employer, Stowe?"

Someone whispered to the judge. "I understand he was denied admittance on the grounds that he would disrupt this hearing."

"I object," the lawyer for the prosecutor's office demanded. "This man is a murderer and a rebel leader who needs to be held under the strictest confinement for this country's safety."

"Objection overruled. Bring Mr. Stowe in here. Attorney Tennison, any man is innocent until he is proven guilty."

The deputy U.S. marshal had a quick conversation with the attorney, and the two men scowled over Stowe's appearance in the court.

"Mr. Stowe, state your name and your business," the judge said when Stowe appeared. "Take the oath. I want to hear your side of the case against Mr. Slocum."

They swore him in, and he gave his name and address and described his business as that of "a buffalo hunter who hires other men to hunt them."

"On the evening of October 28, when this murder occurred, where were you?"

"In Sally Jane's whorehouse sir, immediately across the street from the Oxbow. At the first shot I looked out the window of room four and saw this Hampton on his horse pointing his gun at Slocum, who then shot him in self-defense. Margie, the lady in the room with me, saw it too. I can get fifty men to say the shooting was in self-defense that night. Hampton had already shot another man, who died from his bullet wound."

"Your Honor?" The attorney rose. "This man may well be another agent of this insurgency to overthrow the government of the United States, as Mr. Slocum is, sir."

"Are you an agent of this conspiracy?" the judge asked Stowe.

"No, sir, and neither is Slocum. He is my foreman, of a crew of men who would also testify he never had anything to do with this treason. He has been out there killing buffalo for hides with these men."

"I object, Your Honor. There is a widespread movement in this region to fight the U.S. government. Miles Hampton, a federal officer, was in the process of arresting a man, who resisted him, and Mr. Slocum shot him during that arrest."

"Who did this man work for?" Stowe asked the attorney. "He had no badge that evening that anyone saw. I'd bet a hundred dollars the funeral director found no badge on him. I will have him testify, Your Honor."

"I can prove Hampton was a federal officer on duty at the time of his death," the attorney said.

"Mr. Tennison, my clerk will record the testimony of Mr. Stowe and others in lieu of Mr. Slocum not having an attorney here yet."

"Your Honor, this prisoner must be removed at once. There is a threat by the Washington Revolutionary Army to break him out of jail."

"I doubt they would attack a fort full of soldiers to get this man out."

"Your Honor, they are conspiring to overthrow the entire government of the United States."

"Mr. Tennison, I am sorry, but I think the testimony of Mr. Stowe and others in this case is important for Mr. Slocum to receive a fair trial. We will hold this hearing again on Friday. Until then he is to be held in the fort jail here." He rapped the gavel and dismissed them.

Tennison approached the bench, but the judge refused to hear any more.

Stowe said to Slocum, "Don't worry. We will have that testimony."

The two soldiers took Slocum back to the jail. Light flecks of late snow were swirling in the air when they crossed the fort grounds. Late snows could be deep. It looked to Slocum like it had set in to really bring on a good one; that, plus he had the muscle aches in his body that occurred when a bad storm system came rolling in.

Murty had sent him cinnamon rolls, the jailhouse guard said. He was sure the jail staff had eaten half of them to be certain that there were no files hidden in them. If there were any left, it would be a good thing, because he had missed lunch being in the courtroom hearing and no one had offered to replace it.

For supper they served some navy bean soup and stale bread from the army bakery.

In the middle of the night, he was woken up and handcuffed, then taken to the desk officer of the jail. "This order you have is highly unusual. Judge Morgan's order is to hold him until after the next hearing," the noncom in charge said to one of the deputies escorting Slocum.

"This telegram is from a higher authority than Judge Morgan," the deputy said, holding the telegram before the noncom. "He is an appellate federal judge, and he says we are—the marshals service is—to at once deliver this prisoner to Fort Leavenworth and incarcerate him there in the federal prison. He is a threat to the entire U.S. government and must be held in more secure confinement."

"Hell, he was not going anywhere here, and the judge was not through with him according to my understanding."

"This judge overruled Morgan." The man turned to one of the other lawmen. "Get him dressed in his coat and things. We are taking him out of here at once."

"I need the officer of the day to approve letting you do that, sir."

"I don't need any more shit from you. Get him dressed," he said to his men. "By the power and authority of the federal government vested in me, I am taking this man into my custody. If you want ten years in Leavenworth yourself, then refuse to allow me this man. He is a military prisoner."

They left the jail in a blinding snowstorm and loaded Slocum into a buckboard, wrapped in the blankets he had made them take from his cell. Three men accompanied them on horseback in the worst swirling mass of snow he'd seen in years.

The team was fresh, but this sort of snowy mess would soon wear out even the toughest animals, and the road wasn't easy to follow. He was rocked around in the spring-less bed in back. There was a good chance, in his mind, that he'd not survive the trip and might be murdered to settle their need to eradicate him for some damn high-ranking congressman seeking revenge over his prodigal son's death.

They drove far into the night. With no obvious provisions or firewood, they would have to keep going till they found cover, and in the storm they might drive right by it. Only a handful of venturous souls had tried to homestead out here, in dugouts, and they'd go unseen in this bitter weather unless the team drove over one and fell into it.

They finally stopped to rest their exhausted team and stomped around in the wind and wet snow cussing Slocum.

"Why blame me, boys," he finally said. "Your idiot bosses sent you out in this storm, and I figure we will all be wolf bait within twenty-four hours."

"Shut up," the lead man said. "You will be the first to die, I guarantee you that."

"Any of you knew this Hampton?" he asked them.

He couldn't see them in the dark, snowy night, but more than one grunted no.

"Well, boys, if he was a federal agent, I'm a preacher."

"They say he was spying on that Washington bunch."

"Why shoot a man who was only looking for Spanish gold if he was an agent? The man he shot was a fortune hunter who damn sure had no use for that colonel and his cause. His name was John Trent. He had a wife and family back in Iowa. He told me all that," Slocum lied, "but never said why Hampton shot him."

"He tell you where the gold was?"

"Yeah, that it was buried somewhere west on the Arkansas."

"You get his map?"

"No. I don't chase buried gold."

"Ned, I am going to freeze to death. Why are we out here in this bitter storm? Couldn't this have waited?"

"Hell no, the U.S. attorney general himself said, 'No more fucking around. Get him to Leavenworth.'"

"I bet we get in trouble with Judge Morgan," another man said.

"See how much damn trouble you are to us?" the head man said to him.

"Not me. Blame your boss."

Before dawn they found an empty barn in a letup of the snow and everyone went inside. It was dark in there, but out of the wind at last. The marshals put Slocum's handcuffs around a post, and all went to sleep. The door creaked and

Slocum awoke. A man with a flour sack over his face came into the dim light. A half dozen others with masks and guns drawn also came into the barn. They quickly dispatched the three deputies by striking them over the head, then put their masks on them and tied their feet and legs. Slocum was rubbing his half-frozen hands and sore wrists. Escatar had released him from the cuffs with keys taken from the chief marshal's pocket.

"Your horse is outside and so is a pack mule. Here is your money in a belt that Stowe sent to you. We will take these men's mounts and team and leave them here tied up."

"Thanks. Tell Stowe thanks and Murty too."

"We will," his man said to him.

He soon had the cold canvas belt around his girth and was buttoned up, while Escatar continued, "Then we will wreck the wagon so they can't use it. We are taking their guns, badges, and money and leaving them here. Good luck, *mi amigo*."

"Thanks all of you for saving me. If I can ever help you—"

"No, you have helped us all with our jobs. I will take the outfit out in a few weeks for Stowe. Murty sends her love. She says she will go back to Iowa."

"Thank you, men." He pulled on the gloves they'd brought him and started for his horse and mule.

Someone with a post had smashed out some spokes in the buckboard wheels. In less than ten minutes the marshals' horses were in tow and the men were ready to ride west. Perfect clockwork precision, and Stowe had a good crew to go back to work for him. Murty was going back to Iowa. Slocum would damn sure miss her sweet ass.

He rode north, busting drifts with the gray horse, the black mule tracking with him, as the daylight began to break through the clouds and the snow was over. By noon the south wind joined his back, and the white mess had begun to melt into a slushy mess. He avoided any signs of life and was well on his way to the Republican River and a place where he could rest for a day or two. He sure needed his strength back to go much farther on.

6

After two days of hard riding and fording two swollen smaller rivers, Slocum was nearing the rolling land south of the Republican. He camped in a grove of cottonwoods that night. And a whiskered man in buckskin dropped by his fire and asked to join him.

Slocum offered him a can of peaches and warned him they might still be frozen.

The old man refused his offer, saying he had plenty of jerky of his own. The visitor said his name was Oslo Johansen and he'd been trapping all winter for mink ermine and prime wolf hides.

"I got enough to get some supplies and make it another year. I had me a one-eyed squaw all winter, but she run off just before the last big snow. She tanned a few elk hides. I'd sell you one for ten dollars if you'd want one."

"I always wanted an elk-skin jacket. Folks say they keep you warm and never smother you when the weather turns hotter."

"They are nice if you can find a seamstress. I have one. This hide has only one bullet hole in it."

"Go get it. I may have the money on me somewhere."

The old man made an effort to get up, and on the second try he made it to his feet. Slocum got the money out of one of the pockets in his money belt and snapped it back shut. Damn, Stowe had really packed it full of money. No telling how much he had. He hoped Murty had the gold money, but that might take months. Stowe paid her for cooking each trip, so she should get by. She'd spent little on herself with him—he'd done most of that for her. He shook his head, satisfied that she'd be fine without him.

"Here it is."

"Why, Oslo, this is a wonderful piece of leather," he said, admiring it. The tanning job was so good he could hardly believe it had once been an animal's coat. Snow-white, it might not be the best color for him now that the marshals wanted him too, but he'd have it made into a garment he could wear.

He paid the man and put the elk skin in his pannier.

"I don't guess you're a drinking man," Oslo said when he came back.

"Whiskey, but I don't have any in my bags right now."

"I'll wait. I know an old German down the way here makes some good stuff. Just been so long since I had anything to drink my tongue's about swollen."

"Where will you summer?"

"Oh, up in the mountains where I can eat trout, hang a small deer, and eat it before it rots. Might jerk an elk if I find a squaw to help do it."

"Sounds neat."

"It beats living in a town or plowing crops."

Slocum agreed. But he had more than mental reasons for living out here. He was on the move to avoid the law.

That night he slept well, and the old man was gone when

he awoke near dawn. Strange men wandered the West. Most were friendly and no threat, but crazed killers wandered there as well, men no one knew who murdered helpless individuals for sport and were gone again. The danger always existed in remote places.

The snowmelt had the Republican swollen when Slocum reached it, and he and his animals took the ferry that an old black man cranked across for twenty cents. The wind was from the north, and it sought him riding northwest through the grassy rolling hills.

He reached the Bar N J in mid-afternoon. Dressed in men's jeans and a plaid wool shirt showing her fine breasts' shape under it, Jenny Nelson came out smiling in the doorway. "Where have you been hiding, old man?"

"Oh, places. Looks like spring can't come soon enough around here."

"It sure can't, can it? Get in here and drink some fresh coffee I just made."

"Well my animals can wait a little longer." He caught her in his arms and kissed her. She was a tall woman in her mid-thirties; strong as an ox but very feminine, and they'd had a longtime relationship.

"How has it been going?" she asked him, and her arm on his shoulder, they went inside her log house. The smell of something sweet baking found his nose when she set him in a chair.

Her coffee was Arbuckles' and real smooth. "All right, I guess. How are things going with you?"

"Good. I have a nice set of steers we've wintered. They will be great next summer to market and will keep us in the business. Lots of work to hay them, but my boys are good hands. They've grown a lot since you were here, and they've gotten good at breaking horses. We've sold some. I just fear that homesteaders will shut me out of steer raising in the future.

Oh, and I have been promised delivery late this summer, from a reliable man, of two hundred more light steers to winter."

"It sounds like you and those boys are getting along great."

"We are. Vance is now sixteen and Tom is fourteen. Yes, we sure are, and they will be excited to see that you are here when they get back. They'll want you to help and tell them how they are doing on their horse breaking."

"I will do my best."

"My boys know about our affair. I won't hide it from them unless you feel uncomfortable about it."

"I don't feel uncomfortable ever with you."

"Good. Let's put your animals up. What have you been up to?"

While they stowed his panniers and tack in the harness room, Slocum told her about shooting Hampton in Fort Hayes and the results. He left the treasure part out but told her about his hearing, the plan to send him to Leavenworth Prison, and his eventual escape.

"Oh well, you are no stranger to being on the run, are you?"

He kissed her and held her tight to his body in the barn alleyway. "Hell, no."

"If it was warm enough, I'd take you up in the hayloft like we did years ago."

"I have some fond memories of that loft and you."

"So do I, Slocum."

"I am surprised you haven't found a man by now."

"Some came by. But they wanted to rule my boys like some stern schoolteacher. I couldn't stand that." She frowned and in a harsh mimicking voice said, " 'Them boys need their asses busted twice a day.' " Then she shook her head. "I didn't need them."

"No. And I'll be careful not to be that bad."

She gave him a shove. He knew he could not stay there long, but he aimed to enjoy some time doing things around her ranch.

The boys were coming back from feeding hay to the herd, driving a hayrack with two big black Percheron horses jogging in the jingling harness for the home place.

"Hey, Slocum!" Tom shouted from beside his older brother, who was driving the empty hayrack.

"Our man is back. See her smiling, Tom?"

"Yeah, so am I."

They stopped at the barn and jumped down to hug him and shake his hand. The reunion was good, and the boys were certainly in top physical shape.

"Say," Vance said. "We need to fork on some hay for tomorrow. Join us and we can talk."

"He just got here," their mother said, looking hard at them for wanting to work him so soon.

"We won't kill him, we promise," Tom said, and they all laughed. Tom turned away and went for another pitchfork for Slocum to use.

Slocum scrambled up on the bed, and Tom was back, handing him a fork. And then they were all on board with the big horses headed for the remaining stacks.

"We had a great summer stacking this hay," Vance said.

"And we've worked our asses off this winter feeding it back. We had hoped to have four stacks left for next year, but the way this year is going, we will only have two."

"You guys are doing a man's job here."

"We have money in the bank, and we'll have a good bunch to sell next summer."

"That's super."

"We are breaking some horses. Two are teams and three are saddle horses. These two wasn't very well broke when we bought them, and they are dandies now."

"Great horses."

Pulled in broadside to the stack, Tom tossed Slocum the fork and went off the side. "We have a ladder out back. Vance can stack it on the wagon as fast as we can fork it down."

They fell in trying to cover Vance up, but he was a handy at his job and the rig soon was piled high and loaded. They jumped aboard and rode back to the headquarters. The boys laughed and teased Slocum about coming to see their mom instead of them.

"That isn't even hard to answer. Hell yes."

The big horses were stalled, and they showed him the other teams they had and were breaking.

"That buckskin pair we wanted for her buckboard, but man, they were tough to break. They're still rowdy."

Slocum nodded. "Vance, they will be the toughest team you ever own and the best. Mark my words."

"We almost sold them, but we had a vote and when Mom said not to, we voted with her."

"You guys are lucky. She's a great lady."

"We know that. Where are you headed?"

"Oh, somewhere."

"You ever get tired of riding all over?" Tom asked.

"Not really."

"Tomorrow, we can feed them and then you can give us some tips on these horses we're breaking," Vance said.

"Whatever you guys have to do is fine with me."

In the house and washed up, he could smell the various foods Jenny was cooking in the kitchen.

"Hey, we're glad you came," Tom whispered. "We'll really get some great food."

The boys and Slocum were all laughing.

"What's so funny?" Jenny asked.

Slocum hugged her shoulder where she stood over the cooking range. "You don't want to hear it."

He and the boys laughed some more about it.

After the meal, they played cards for matches. Vance won big-time in draw poker. Finally the boys went upstairs to bed after banking the stove. Slocum and Jenny sat on the couch and kissed until she led him off to her bedroom. They undressed and she put on a knee-length nightgown, He wore a nightshirt she had for him. Under the covers, they soon were busy making love. Different than his last, giggling partner, her body meshed with his, and they soon reached a high that fell off into more kissing. He slept until she woke him before dawn.

"Tonight," she whispered in his ear and kissed him sweetly. "You never lose your touch to arouse me. I know that you are on the run again. But thanks, Cowboy, for stopping—you really please me when you do."

Then she quickly dressed in the darkness and went to start breakfast. He got up and dressed, then went outside in the cold and pissed. Spring must not be coming this year. Many years they had broken the garden and planted potatoes and cabbage by this time.

Jenny went to town later in the week and returned upset. "They don't look like you, but they have reward posters in the post office and even one nailed on the Collins store, out front. I tried to ignore them, but they have a five-hundred-dollar reward on them for you, dead or alive."

"That's the most valuable I have ever been. Anyone talking to you about me?"

She shook her head. "I don't think anyone has put you and me together much in the past five years. Your visits since then have all been sweet but short."

"I don't want to bring you any harm. I'll shoe my animals tomorrow and ride on."

"We can help you do that," Vance said. "I hate for that to happen, but I am concerned someone may connect you to us. Five hundred dollars is lots of money today, and someone could rush out here to get you."

"I agree. Well it has been a nice visit with you, Jenny, and both you guys. You really are growing up into men."

"Slocum, we may have been little, but I recall what you did for Mom after they shot Pa. We'd not be living on this ranch and having what we have if you hadn't cleaned up that bunch of outlaws that ran over this country back then."

Tom nodded. "That Jim Blocker shot Pa in the back to get her for himself. But she wasn't taking him on a bet. And I can recall being scared enough I pissed in my pants. You don't ever forget that. And you've come by many times, to help and teach me and Vance how to do things. Hell, we'd hide you in the storm cellar if we had to."

"That congressman lost a prodigal son, and he blames all that on me. They didn't want me to have a fair trial. It was all set up to railroad me into a hanging. I may never clear my name from this frame-up, but there's not much I can do but keep them shagging my tail till they get tired of it."

"It's damn shame though," Vance said between bites of his pancakes dripping with sugar syrup. "But come back, we'll feed you."

Their mother shook her head, looking close to tears. "Slocum knows he's always welcome here. He's the man."

Then Jenny rushed off, and both boys dropped their chins. Vance finally said, "Don't worry. It is always like that when you leave. We can comfort her after you ride on."

They worked horses all day after haying the steers. The cattle all looked good, and many were licking the hair on their sides, a sure sign to Slocum that they were gaining weight. The black horse was three and soon to be part of a matched team. The mare was two, and while she was more brown than black, they'd make a good farm team.

"Whoever gelded him did it wrong," Slocum told the boys. "It won't ruin him, but he still thinks at times he's a stallion. A summer of mowing hay will drain some of that out of him."

Tom agreed. "That's real important how you castrate a horse, isn't it?"

"Yes it is. How old was he when they cut him?"

"This past spring."

"Then he'd probably bred some mares, or tried to, before he was cut."

"Some old man did it before we bought him."

The gelding had his head high, and the strong wind flagged his wavy mane. His whinnying made his whole body shake.

"Keep working with him. He'll soon discover his balls are gone," Slocum said in a teasing tone.

Both boys laughed

"Glad he didn't get mine," Vance said and laughed. Tom agreed.

Next day they reshod his gray and the mule. It had warmed up, and most of the snow was gone except in the deep shady spots. A wonderful special final night in bed with the amorous body of Jenny, her long legs and fine boobs to kiss and taste, had closed the curtain down on Slocum's visit. At dawn he rode off to the north, after kissing her hard and shaking her young men's calloused hands. He could have stayed there for a long time.

She'd whispered something she told him she'd read on the wanted poster—*He may be riding a tall gray horse.*

7

The Nebraska line was a visible scar he crossed over, marked by a crude sign using NEBR on the first line, ASKA on the second line. He knew where some trash hung out in the Platte River Brakes, but for now he wasn't going there. A two-day ride or more was still ahead for him to get where he wanted to go, but the land was gently rolling grassy plains. This was Pawnee land, and he intended to stop at their large village.

When he drew closer to the great half-underground lodge that they all lived in as one big community, he spoke to a woman going for water.

"I am looking for Three Bear. Is he here?"

She wrinkled her nose, then checked to be sure that no one was close. "He has a new wife. I think he is busy servicing her right now."

Slocum nodded and thanked her like that was the answer he'd expected. Some Indians were very frank in what they said—and there was a tinge of jealousy in her tone of voice. Before she'd gone ten steps, she called to him and waited until he had turned the gray toward her. "White man, my name is Swan Woman. I am a widow."

"My name is Slocum. I have no wife."

She was wrapped tight in the trade blanket, and a sweet smile crossed her copper lips. "I will take you to Three Bear." With that she hung her metal pail on his pack mule, and with the fringed bottom of her dress slapping her shapely calves above her moccasins, she hurried to be beside his horse. He dropped his arm down for her and swung her up behind the cantle. This wasn't her first horse ride double, he decided, as she settled in place hugging him freely.

"Where did you come from?" she asked.

"Kansas."

She laughed. "Everyone comes from Kansas."

"I visited a family I knew on the Republican River."

She leaned around a little. "Where is your home?"

"Far south is where I was raised." The memory of those days nagged at him, the war years and the aftermath exploding his dreams and completely devastating his future. But he had no intention of opening up about that now.

"If you're taking me to find my friend, what will you do for water?"

"Drink from the family next to me's supply."

"Oh, yes, the Pawnee way is 'What you have I have also.'" She laughed. "You are no stranger to our ways."

"What happened to your man?"

"He was killed fighting the Sioux with the army."

"Bad thing to happen to you."

"Maybe, maybe not. Today I met a man with a fine horse and good mule. After you see Three Bear, where will you go?"

"I plan to go to the Brakes next."

"Is there room for a squaw to go along?"

"I'd buy her a horse to ride."

"Better yet. Yes, I would go with you. Stop here. I will

go find him for you." She slipped off the gray's butt to her feet, straightened her blanket, and went proudly inside the great lodge's entrance. Curious small boys and girls pointed at Slocum and his horse. They wore only short leather shirts and were all naked below that. Saved changing diapers, he decided. Lined up, they giggled and pointed at the stranger in their presence.

A large woman soon rounded them up, scolding them in Pawnee for pointing at him. The last small boy stuck his tongue out at Slocum and made him laugh. Lots of traffic going in and out, then Swan Woman reappeared with his friend Three Bear, a burly-chested giant of a man wearing an eagle-bone vest and a breechcloth.

"Ah, Slocum," he roared. "What brings my friend to here?"

"To see my friend Three Bear, and to laugh about old times," Slocum said, coming down off his horse.

"There is not much to laugh about. They want us to move to Indian Territory. It is too damn hot down there. The corn won't grow as tall, and there would be people we hate there and don't agree to have as our neighbors." He shook his head warily. "Why down there, do you suppose?"

"I am not the white father, nor can I speak for him." They hugged and then shook hands.

"I am sorry. You and I are like small feathers that fell from a hummingbird wing."

"Smaller than that. Good to see you and learn that you are still sowing oats in young women."

Three Bear laughed. "Nothing is secret in this great house. Nothing. Come. We will find some good food I know you can eat."

Slocum stopped and thanked Swan Woman.

"I will watch your animals. They need a drink and to graze. You can find me down by the river." She used her slender hand to point out the direction.

"Thank you, Swan Woman. I will join you later."

Her head bowed, she nodded and went off with his stock.

"Ah, my horny friend is only here a few minutes, and already he has a pretty widow woman corralled. No different than ever. Come and meet my men and some more woman."

"One at a time is enough for me," Slocum said and followed Three Bear inside.

"Ah, but you are not a chief. They expect more from me. Now I have three wives. I take the daughters from other chiefs to show I am like a brother to them."

"I understand. You must have had enough food for all of your people, and now winter is near over."

"We still have food, but we already planted some corn early in case the next season is dry."

"I had some bad luck in Kansas. I have been hunting buffalo for almost a year down there. Had a good crew. Came out of a saloon one night and saw a man shoot another in cold blood. Then he turned his gun on me. I shot him in self-defense. But he was a Washington congressman's son, and they said I murdered him. I was being rushed off to federal prison without a trial. My men freed me and so now I am a fugitive."

"Oh, the government men, they have ways, don't they?"

"Like sending you and your people to another land." Slocum shook his head.

Soon men starting coming inside, and some came over to sit on the floor. On the outer ring women were seated, some nursing babies. Others were enforcing a "sit down and be silent" rule on their tagalongs.

"This man is my friend, Slocum," Three Bear told the group. "He and I have hunted and we have fought together many times. Once a war party of Sioux were trailing us. There were maybe two handfuls of them yipping and screaming on our tail. He said for us to ride up this steep hill and we could face them off. I didn't believe him. He had two rifles—a buffalo gun and a Sharps .50-caliber, and he used the Sharps first. He told me to save my ammunition, that they were too far away for my gun. We were on our bellies watching them come toward us. A warrior with his face painted black, who had been shouting at them to hurry and kill us. Slocum took aim and shot the war leader off his horse.

"Then he reloaded as they milled and made some dust. The chief came out screaming next, and Slocum sent him to where all good Sioux go. Two of their leaders gone, they picked their dead up and one showed us his ass. The dumbest one in the tribe. Slocum shot him too. They rode away without him."

The men were laughing.

"He is good man. The women say they have time to have a feast tonight. Warm enough we can build a big fire outside to celebrate my friend's visit."

A cheer went up, and everyone shook Slocum's hand.

Finally he spoke to his friend. "I am going to rest for a while. I will be there when the drums begin."

"Much dancing. Have big time. We need to laugh more anyway."

"Good. I will come and laugh with you."

They hugged, and Slocum went to Swan and his horses. He soon learned they were farther away than he had thought she'd go, and finally, over the next rise he spotted the gray hobbled and the mule as well. She'd even unsaddled the stock and set his panniers off to the side.

He found her under some walnut trees in the sunshine, for warmth, sitting cross-legged on his bedroll. He dropped down beside her and stretched out.

"You didn't have to do all that."

"I said I'd care for them."

"You did good." On his belly he chewed on a long grass stem. "You have any children?"

"They both died. They took sick and then died. I was very sad."

"I keep asking you questions that hurt your heart, don't I?"

She shook her head and put her black braids over her shoulders. "I am enjoying talking to you. You are different than most white men."

"How is that?"

"You don't talk in broken English to me. You don't suggest I am a whore who needs you."

"What if I did?"

"I would think you were teasing me." She laughed. "I know why Three Bear likes you."

"Why is that?"

"You talk to him like he is your brother. What will you do in the Brakes?"

"Maybe live for a while. See, I have a price on my head, and men will come looking for me in time. But every day I can just be a man and live in peace, I am grateful for."

"You look like a man in peace today." She stood and began to take the deerskin dress off over her head, exposing her brown legs, then the black pubic area, her flat belly, and the pear-shaped breasts, as he rose on his knees to help her.

"May we get under the covers? There is no scent of another woman in them."

He pulled off his boots while she laid her dress on the panniers. She was a neatly made tall woman. He let her get under the blankets and then he undressed. At last he joined her and considered the treasures he held under the blankets. A willing, supple woman who molded to his body and whom he kissed, growing excited about their path ahead. Indian women hardly knew kissing, but they soon learned, as she did. Then they fell in a whirlpool of kisses, with his flesh against her muscled body. Soon connected as one, they worked each other hard.

After a nap, they straightened up, redressed, and went to the festivities. She wore his many-times-rained-on felt hat. She asked if he minded and he shook his head. "Wear it as long as you want."

He knew that for her to show up wearing his headgear let everyone there know that he was hers. And she walked proud in her deerskin dress, the fringe wrapping around her calves, the hat a little too big, covering her forehead, with her braids trailing down her back.

She said, "You need an eagle feather or two for it to be a lucky hat."

"No, it is a lucky hat because I have you to wear it."

She tried to see out of it, to look at him after his statement. Then she hugged his waist. "Tonight I am proud I met you."

He joined his friend, and she went to help the other women, but did not relinquish his hat.

Three Bear laughed at the sight of him hatless. "She already scalped him."

Slocum laughed and joined him. "Women will do that to you."

"Oh, how well I know."

"I need a good horse for her to ride. She says she is going with me."

"I can get you one."

"I will pay you for it."

"I will give you one."

"No. Sell it to me."

Slocum finally gave up. That hardheaded Pawnee wasn't taking any money for the horse. So he found Swan Woman, and they joined a stomping line of dancers. Women teased him, and he laughed, not understanding half what they said to him.

Lots of fire-roasted meat left them all with shiny lips from eating the grease. Little ones were herded off to bed eventually, and the night dancing became more exciting. The chanting grew louder, and the movement was like a great serpent snaking around. Slocum forgot about everything else but the willowy Swan Woman and him—isolated as if they danced inside a huge bubble floating among so many others but in their own private world.

At last they ran off into the night, to their own cave under the blankets and stars, to make love with a newfound fierceness. Slocum felt better than he had in weeks.

The ox yoke on his neck had been lifted for one night anyway.

8

They left before the sun came up on the third day. Swan rode a nice paint mare with a three-month-old paint horse colt still nursing on her. With the mule in her care, they left for the northwest. Slocum carried a Winchester across his lap. The colt was a strong one, so Slocum had no worry about him keeping up. Swan rode a blanket saddle with stirrups and a girth. She could hurl herself on the mare's back in a flurry of fringe and be ready to race when her butt hit the blanket.

He stopped at a small store at a crossroads on the prairie. Inside he found a good beaver hat that he liked and that fit him. He paid the man after some dickering and then put the felt one on her head. She smiled contentedly and tied the strings he never used, to save it if the wind tried to steal it from her.

They flushed prairie chickens as they rode away. To not lose a high-crowned hat in the prairie country was a learned art. One adjusted, without thought, the tilt of one's head to the various veins of wind. She must have had that skill, he decided, for she never lost it that day, though the tied strings surely helped. In no hurry they jogged the horses some and walked a lot. Mid-afternoon, they made camp at a spring full of watercrests. The water was cool and sweet. They found enough fuel to make a fire, and with some help from him, she made coffee with boiled ground beans. The big horses and mule were hobbled so they grazed while the colt lay down in the sunshine to absorb it. He'd made it fine, but Slocum supposed it had been a long day for him anyway.

"Have you ever been to St. Louis?" she asked.

"A few times."

"Did you like it?"

"I don't enjoy cities. They are confining. No hunting. People live too close. Gangs control areas. Children are abused. Forced to work instead of play."

She nodded.

"Why?"

"I only wondered. I heard stories about large boats like houses that belch smoke and have paddle wheels behind."

"Riverboats?"

"Yes. Are they all right?"

"Sure."

"You ever ride a smoking one on an iron trail?"

"You mean a train?"

"Yes."

"Lots of times."

"Was it fun?" She poured the two of them coffee in tin cups.

"Not the laughing kind."

"I talk too much. But I always wondered about things I had never seen and what they would be like."

"Knowledge is what fuels your education."

"I never went to school. Am I too old to ever learn how to read?"

"No. You can learn how."

"Being an Indian does not stop you from reading?" She

busied herself, on her knees, making fry bread and getting the skillet hot.

"No one can stop you from reading."

"Good. I will learn how. You are a strange white man. You are not a priest, not a minister, yet you speak about things I never expected to learn and you say them truthful. A Pawnee husband can't read and don't care that he can't read. So his woman does not need to know how to read and be ahead of him."

"Some white men think like that too."

They ate beans with salt and pepper on them, plus the fry bread. She made enough for their next morning meal as well. Then they listened to whip-poor-will making love calls and later went to sleep.

That night Slocum also heard the frogs croaking. Spring would soon be there.

Two days later, with no incidents so far, they met a traveling photographer with his wagon. The man's name was Beecher, and he said that for a dollar he would make a picture of them standing together. He also wanted one with Swan Woman's colt if he would stand still.

She looked at his examples and nodded she wanted one made.

Slocum said he would buy one for her.

"You must stand very still for a long time. If you move your face, then it will be a blur." Turning to Slocum, he said, "Hold your rifle in your arm."

"What will we look like?" she asked.

"The plainsman and his squaw," Beecher replied.

He took the picture with his great box camera, with bellows like they used on a forge, set up perched on a tripod.

Beecher acted excited when he removed the plate. "I believe I have it."

He went inside his wagon and was gone and gone. At last

he emerged waving a small item. They ran over to see the results. Sure enough he had them on the silver, gray, and white card about the size of a postcard. There were Swan Woman and Slocum standing side by side, him holding the rifle and her under his brown hat. They made a real pair, Slocum mused.

"Oh, this is wonderful," she cried. "I have never had such a thing before."

Slocum paid the man and they rode on, with her completely entranced by the entire thing.

The next day he stopped at a store to get some items that they were near out of, and she tended the animals while he was inside. No one else was there when he went into the store that smelled of harness oil, grain, and dry goods. After he paid the man for the spices and baking powder, he heard lots of noises and the mule braying in the confusion outside.

Must have been fifty pack mules all braying at once, and some whiskered bear was kissing a kicking Swan. He held her arms in his massive hands, and her moccasined feet were off the ground. His efforts had knocked the hat onto her back.

"Put that woman down," Slocum shouted, running out in the daylight and clutching the cocked Colt in his right fist. That crazy madman had his woman!

The man, under a near-shapeless hat, whirled around still holding Swan Woman in the air. "Who in the fuck are you— Slocum? That you?"

"Put her down."

"I am, I am. Put that damn gun away, man. I should have known she belonged to you. No one else could have found such a pretty Pawnee and talked her into a having a honeymoon with him. I have been out there so damn long my balls are moldy. What are you doing way up here?"

"That's my business, Pistol Pete."

The big man swept off his shapeless hat and bowed to

Swan Woman. "So sorry, ma'am, but you are so beautiful I could not resist your charming attractions. You are so beautiful and so lucky to have him."

Obviously not moved by his apology, she wiped off both of her sleeves where he had gripped her and wore a scowl of disgust on her brown face. Then she put the hat back on and strode to Slocum's side. "I never encouraged him to do that."

"Hell, if you'd been a goat he'd have grabbed you the same way."

"I never—"

He knew she was upset and he whispered, "I know that."

She nodded and crossed her arms over her breasts—still seething mad. Then he could really smell the stinking buffalo hides on the pack mules. These men were returning hunters. Dressed in heavy coats despite the day's warm air, they stunk worse than a stagecoach-stop outhouse.

"Boys, this is the great Slocum," Pete said. "He was southern fried as a boy and in the war he was a captain. But he's a well-known outlaw now like the rest of us, on the run from federal agents and those Pinkerton pricks."

Slocum looked at the black faces of two ex-slaves, the brown faces of two Mexicans and two breeds, and the pale rat face of a runt Slocum knew as Weasel—who together made up Pete's gang. They were either seated on saddle mules or standing around looking for more than one store and probably a whorehouse as well.

"How you been?" Pete asked Slocum.

"Fine. How about yourself?"

"Killing buff. Only honest work we can find. But we are going to find us a hide buyer and some white whores and plow their fields up."

"I understand. Well, plenty of good luck doing both." He motioned for Swan Woman to get on her mare. "We're going to see if the Rockies still sparkle in the sunlight."

Slocum and Swan, on their horses with the mule and colt

following, left Pete and his men there on their galled raw mules, watching with hard-eyed looks. When they were beyond earshot, Slocum rode in close. "Sorry."

"No need to be. Those men give all white men a bad name. I am glad you didn't kill him, 'cause all those other men might have killed you."

"It was not a matter of who died."

"I knew that too. I am grateful."

"When you live out here on the edge, those kind of people show up."

She nodded. For a long ways she was silent, and when they stopped to camp, she stood with him holding her tight for a long time. Then she hurried around making camp and acting like herself again. Her meal cooking, she sat beside him on the bedroll.

"Will we go see the sparkling Rockies?"

"I just said that to make conversation with him. It was none of his business where we went. Now he will say to others he saw that Slocum in Nebraska and he was going to the Rockies. That will become gossip on the lips of men seeking favor or money for that news when they're contacted by lawmen or detectives."

"That is like seeding corn, isn't it? They will go look for the stalks?"

"Exactly."

She acted smug over her discovery, and they ate more beans and fry bread made in a skillet. He opened a can of peaches, and they shared the juice and fruit in it.

By bedtime she was back to acting herself again and they made love. No way to guess her age, but he felt she was maybe twenty or even a year or two older. He enjoyed her energy and dedication to him, along with her willowy body.

They rose before dawn, ate oatmeal with raisins and brown sugar, drank coffee, and rode on. They reached the Brakes, and Slocum knew a few of the men in the scattered cabins and dugouts. To him they were all too harsh to be around, and so they crossed the Platte and rode west on the great wagon road. It was before the grass broke dormancy, so this was still a barren area due to overgrazing by the emigrants and the train tracks that had now been laid in that place.

Slocum knew a man who raised horses north of there, and so he rode to see him. But he found that John Henry's cabin and corrals had been burned to the ground some time earlier. Obviously it was the work of an Indian war party. He was disappointed that his old friend was either dead or had moved on. They found a neighbor woman at home a few miles west. Her wash streaming on rope lines, she looked at them with suspicion in her eyes when Slocum reined up.

"Ma'am, sorry to bother you," he said.

A tall, raw-boned woman, she swept the blond hair from her face and squinted in the sunshine at him. "What do you need?"

"What happened to John Henry? I just came from there."

"The goddamn Sioux attacked him last summer. He's still alive, but moved to Ogallala. He lives with his cousin out there."

"Bad deal."

"Me, my husband, and his brother were under attack for half a day, but we killed five of them and they never got us. They finally left and the next day the army arrived. But John was coming home the day before. He was alone and they wounded him, and then they trailed his mares and two stud horses away. I sure miss him. He was a nice man toward me and all my family."

Slocum thanked her and tossed his head to Swan that they were leaving. The woman's name was Emma, and Slocum knew John Henry had frequented her. Her and those two men she spoke about were having a rough time making it—so Emma entertained men like John to make their ends meet. They were her egg money—she didn't have any chickens.

He and Swan never stopped in any town, but rather camped away from faces, until they were near the home of another man Slocum knew and so they rode to his place. Curly Manard was breaking a horse in a round corral when they rode onto his ranch. He had the horse running in a circle, but he stopped and climbed up on the fence, still holding his air rifle. He shot the horse in the flank with BBs until the horse quit trying to escape and came to him.

Seated on the top rail, he removed his hat and swiped his wet forehead on his sleeve.

"Afternoon, ma'am," he said, like Slocum was not even with her. "I'm so glad you dropped in. My name is Curly and my head ain't as curly as it used to be, but you can see this. Who is this man you brought along?"

She straightened her back and smiled. "My name is Swan Woman. He goes by Slocum."

"My, what is a famous lady like you doing riding with such a low-bellied hombre?"

"All I could get." She jumped off her horse. Curly set down the rifle and ran to hug her, then swung her around in a wide circle.

"Well I feel sorry for you." He set her down and kissed her forehead.

"Crazy, ain't he, Swan?" Slocum asked her.

She shrugged and fought a smile. "Better than most."

Slocum laughed and hugged his friend. They had lots to say to each other, so with him on one side of her and Curly on the other, they herded Swan to the house and inside it.

Slocum had never thought about it, but she had never been inside a farmhouse before in her life, and she was totally struck by all of it. She whirled around trying to take it all in at once.

"What a wonderful place."

Her obvious awe of everything made both men smile. She was in a heaven on earth, far, far from the smoky crowded round house at home. The fireplace, the range in the kitchen portion, the hand pump in the sink that produced water with only a small effort on the handle—she gazed around at everything. Then, with her butt backed to the sink, she sighed. "Where is your wife?"

"She died last winter," Curly said. "They said pneumonia."

"I am so sorry. I too have a sad story. My husband was killed fighting as an army scout. Then such a thing as took your wife took both my children."

"Then you ended with this scoundrel Slocum?"

"I chose him when he came to our lodge to see Three Bear. He gave me his hat and said we must ride to see his friends."

"I am so glad you came, Swan."

"May I fix you some food?"

"I can show you how to use the range."

"I fear I might burn your house down."

"No fear."

Slocum hung his hat on a peg, then retrieved it, recalling that he had animals to put up.

"I will come help you," Swan said.

"No, you learn how to cook in here. I can put things up."

She accepted his answer and turned back so Curly could show her how to fire up the range. Slocum smiled at them as Curly showed her more things. He went outside and unsaddled the animals, then put his panniers and the pack-saddle in Curly's harness shed. The animals he turned into a corral with hay and water. They rolled on their backs to stop the itching where the saddles had been.

Satisfied, he went back inside and hung up his jacket and hat. He sat down to read some newspapers. In the back of the Denver newspaper he came across a story with the headline MURDERER OF MISSOURI CONGRESSMAN'S SON STILL ON THE LOOSE. The story read:

> U.S. Marshal Craig Jensen reported that the man, guilty of murdering Miles Hampton, a federal agent, had escaped federal agents while being taken to Leavenworth Prison to be hung for his heinous crime. In a well-planned attack by agents from the rogue government of Washington, the prisoner escaped and all the federal agents were badly beaten and left to die tied up in ropes in freezing temperatures.
>
> John Slocum is being sought at this time with a five-hundred-dollar reward to be paid for him alive or dead. Slocum is thirty-three, a former Confederate captain, and has been connected to this rogue government Washington. He is dark-haired and six feet tall. The following drawing is ten years old, but he looks like this today according to the agents who arrested him. Consider him armed and dangerous.

"You find that?" Curly asked.

"I was never convicted or even tried. I had a hearing coming, and those agents rushed me out of Fort Hayes to take me to Leavenworth. This boy's father is a powerful congressman. They said the son was a federal agent, which no one believes. He was treasure hunting and shot a man probably because he knew too much and Hampton feared he would beat him to the loot."

"Sounds like you fell into another bowl full of shit."

"I did."

"Where is she from?"

"Swan is a Pawnee. You heard her story."

"Yes. She is a nice woman."

"She yearns to read."

Curly nodded.

"We have been coming this way the past few weeks while they really look for me back there. I am thinking I might slip out of sight into the north."

"Then how can you clear this up?"

"I don't know. While I waited for an attorney to come out there, we convinced the federal judge at Fort Hayes to hear witnesses to the shooting. He was listening, but the marshals didn't want that to be told in open court, so they hustled me out of there and on the way to Leavenworth before that happened. I felt they'd shoot me for trying to escape, as an excuse for killing me. My friends figured it out, followed, ran down the marshals, and whacked them all over the head, tied them up, and sent me packing."

"You were damn lucky. But how will this ever be solved?"

"I don't know. Somewhere there is a lawyer with the money and power enough to close that case."

"I don't know him. Do you?"

"No."

Swan fed them supper and smiled. "Your friend has a wonderful house."

"I know we have not spoken about it, but I may have to leave you here with Curly. I have more bad news about them wanting to arrest me."

She nodded, looking very upset.

"My friend Curly has a nice ranch here. He would like you to stay here. He understands Indian women. His wife who died was a full-blood Cheyenne. Besides being my good friend he is a good man."

"If he does not like me, how will I get home?"

"He will return you to your people."

Curly raised his hand. "I swear I will take you back there."

"I will be sad. I have lost so much."

"I am sad too, but they are pushing hard to bring me down. But here you will have a secure place, and he will teach you to read I promise you."

"When will you leave me?"

"Tonight."

She swallowed hard. "I understand."

"Won't you be happy in this fine house?"

She nodded. "If I had you too. But I will try to please him."

"Good." Turning to Curly, he added, "She has a picture of us standing together."

Curly nodded. "Good, she will have that for a memory of you."

Slocum agreed and said, "I'm sorry to make this such a grave meal. Your first made on a stove top too."

"I have had few metal pots in my life. I have boiled water in hides with hot rocks. When I left with you and saw that small Dutch oven, I almost cried. So yes, he has a wonderful house with no smoke in my place and very private walls."

"You will do well here in his care, Swan." He reached over and patted her hand.

After dark, he loaded up and rode north.

9

He left leading his mule and rode across the bridge spanning the Platte, heading north in the starlight. No close calls, but the hair on his neck stuck straight up riding through the drunks staggering in the Ogallala main street in the night. North of the river at last, he trotted his animals under the stars. His plan was to make it to the Fort Robinson area next. He'd covered lots of Nebraska and was in the grassy country on a little-traveled road when he met a man carrying his saddle on his shoulder and walking.

"You walk far?" He stopped his gray.

"Too far. My horse gave out back up the road. I had to destroy him." The youth, in his late teens, looked weary.

"Where are you headed?"

"Colorado. I figure I might find work down there."

"Let's camp. I have some food we can fix and you can rest a little."

"Hey, mister, no one has offered me a thing. I'm indebted to you. And that is a great gray horse—" Then he stopped.

"You . . . you're the guy they want for killing that congressman's son."

"I shot him in self-defense."

"Boy, your wanted poster is all over the damn country. Says you were convicted of murder and sentenced to hang."

"That is all a lie. You don't believe me, you can hike on down the road."

"Hey, mister, I lied about my horse. I stole a horse up north and figured they'd recognize him in Ogallala, so I let him loose and started out walking, not knowing I was over thirty miles from there."

Slocum laughed at the young man. "I have a plan. You ride my gray horse clear down into Colorado. I'll make you a bill of sale for him. Don't stop so anyone sees you for long, and then strike out. You should get clear down there, and some will think it was me went through. I'll pay you twenty dollars besides."

"Holy shit, mister, I can ride him to the Mexican border for that. Good, but what will you do with this camp stuff?" He looked around at the mule and the panniers.

"I guess leave it. Better than being picked off because I have it."

The kid agreed. "But a damn shame."

"I've had to lose more than that to save my hide before. We can split what we can use and tow sack it."

"Sounds good. Am I glad I met you, mister—"

"Slocum."

"Jerry Kane."

"Now, let's fix supper."

"Yes, sir."

The preparation went well. Afterward they split the cans of tomatoes and peaches left and some other items. Slocum kept the coffee and the candy. The next morning they ate well and parted. The mule was not well broke to rein, but after some arguing, Slocum won and he trotted him off north. Kane rode south as the decoy with a bill of sale from "Andrew Thomas" for the gray horse.

The mule was extremely tiring to ride or drive for Slocum, but in two days he was at an isolated ranch in a great swale, with lots of wet land around it, near the South Dakota line.

A handsome woman in her late twenties came to the door in a blue dress.

"Good day." He removed his hat. "My name's Slocum. Could I buy a meal?"

Amused, she covered her mouth and shook her head in disbelief looking at him. Finally recovered, she stepped outside and leaned her back to the door frame. "I have had many folks stop by looking for a handout. But you are the first one ever, mister, to offer to pay for it."

"Can I buy it?"

"Hell, no. Get off your mule and I'll wrangle you up something for free. I'm Glenna, Glenna Russell. I gave you my name. Now, who are you?"

"Thanks, Slocum is mine."

"Just Slocum, huh?"

"Yeah, it makes it easier."

Glenna turned and showed her fingers over her shoulder for him to come inside after her.

"Good." He hitched the mule at the rack and started for the house. On the porch he stuck his hat on a rack and washed his hands and face in the basin. Then he dried them on the sack towel available and stepped inside the neat cabin.

"You have a very nice place here," he said to her back while she was working on the wood range.

She looked back. "You can sit at the table. You've been on the road awhile."

"I probably could use a bath and a shave. But food seems like to me to be a little more important."

"When did you eat last?"

"Oh, yesterday I had my last can of peaches."

"I have some beef stew I am heating. You must be on the run."

"I am."

"Well, you aren't Jesse James. I have seen fuzzy pictures of him."

"No, ma'am. I recently shot a man in self-defense in Kansas after he shot a man in cold blood and then turned his gun on me. Only thing is he was the prodigal son of a congressman. I have never been on trial and they call me a convicted criminal."

She served him a bowl of hot stew. "I'll cut you some sourdough bread. It's still hot."

"Thank you, Glenna."

"You don't have to keep thanking me. Any man rode a mule that far is tough as anyone I know. I saw right off he is not a saddle mule."

Between spoons of his stew, Slocum managed to say, "My gray horse was too famous to ride any longer."

"I said you were tough." She poured him some fresh-smelling coffee.

"Your husband around?"

"He's dead. He had a horse wreck and died two days later over a year ago. My brother Jon and I own this place."

"I am sorry."

"No need to be. I have not cried a tear. He chose a horse that morning I told him was too tough for him, but he rode off on him anyway. I tried to save him from dying. He never listened. What more could I have done?"

"I guess he made his own decision." Her stew was delicious.

"He did that." Sounding as if she was through talking about her late husband, she said, "I have a sheepherder shower. If there is not a posse right on your trail, I'll give you a towel and soap. But I will not tell you that the water is hot."

"I would be grateful."

"And I am going to get you some clothes that may fit you so I can wash those you have lived in so long." She shook her head as if she couldn't believe his situation.

"There are not any bath houses on the back roads between here and Fort Hayes."

"Well, you've found one today. You want more stew?"

"I'd take some more of your great sourdough bread, butter, and that chokecherry jam."

"Oh, bragging will get you more." She jumped up to fill his order.

After he ate three more slices, she pointed out the way and he trekked off for the shower. The water in the barrel overhead was certainly not warm, but he felt good shedding the dirt and stink associated with his long mule ride to here. His plans included buying a horse to ride when he could find one.

Dry and dressed in borrowed clothing, he put his gun belt on again and then headed for the cabin. Nice place for a ranch, nestled under the hill; a small, clear creek ran by it, no doubt spring-fed, and surrounding it were big cottonwoods that soon would leaf out and a large garden spot in the alluvial riverbed. The place was well fenced to keep out vermin and plowed ready to plant potatoes and greens. It all looked serene—pens, haystacks, mowing equipment, and two teams of big draft horses in the corral. Her husband had left her with a nice place.

"Looks like Jon's clothes fit you all right. Him and Carter will be back here in an hour or so. We have some trouble with a pushy guy named Horace Garvin. Moved in here because they ran him out of Texas some folks say. He gets awful pushy, thinks he owns the entire range. He's run off some homesteaders over on the river. So we go with two men whenever we leave the ranch. Carter is a good old man. He's tough, and Jon can and will stand up for himself, but they've got some hard-core sumbitches over at the Two G Bar. His foreman, Buck Sears, is some tough outlaw, seems to me."

"Has this Garvin threatened folks you know about?"

"Yeah, he had one woman in tears. Her husband was gone when they came by telling her to leave. They ain't left, but they're real concerned. Another woman shot at them with a shotgun. Two of them got bucked off their horses when the pellets hit their horses' butts."

"Sounds like they need a few more lessons."

"Would you be able to do something? I know you've been around, and I wondered what you could try on them." She folded her arms over her chest, busy overseeing the cooking on the range. "Sit down at the table. We don't have lots of furniture."

"No problem. I'd hang a dummy on the ranch crossbar and pin a sign on him: GO HOME OR DIE."

She began laughing. "How hard is that?"

"Some old clothes stuffed with hay, a pillowcase with a mouth and eyes painted on it, and a rope knotted and all around his neck."

"By damn that might shake them some."

"It won't run off the real tough guys, but it will thin out the dumb ones."

"Is that posse real close to your tail?"

"I hope they're looking for me in Colorado."

"We could pay you to stay a few days and get that going." She'd come to sit across from him at the table.

"Just sell me a horse."

"Hell, we can give you one if you can get these guys going on this send-them-home deal. What else can we do?"

"Don't they all go to town and get drunk?"

"Yeah, Saturdays. They do that over at Buttercup. At the O'Riley Bar. What do we do then?"

"Cut some cinches, tie some tin cans on their horses' tails in long chains, and set off some Chinese firecrackers."

"What would you do next?"

"Next I'd set some explosives and blow up the corral that holds their horses and scatter them to hell and gone."

"You've done this before?"

"Maybe. But I know it will thin down his ruffians in a hurry."

"I can't wait to tell Jon about this. He's been itching to run them off, but see we'd never thought of all that." She reached over and clasped the top of his hands with her own. "We've been needing you for some time."

"Thanks. Next time I'll stay longer." He teased her.

She drew a deep breath up her slender nose. It had been broken sometime earlier, but that only added to her appeal to him—*tomboy*. He figured she'd been thrown off a pony or maybe a horse. No telling, but she was a nice-looking woman—tough-acting, but she'd had to be to live out here and survive.

Jon and Carter arrived, and Slocum and Glenna went outside to see how their day had gone. A warm wind was blowing out of the south, and the two looked weary. Jon was in his early twenties and Carter was close to forty, with gray sideburns and sharp blue eyes.

"This is Slocum. His story is too long to tell out here. You guys have any trouble today?"

"Not that we couldn't handle," Carter said, sounding mad. "Nice to meetcha, Slocum. As for our trouble, we pulled a wild cow out the mud, and when we got her out, two of his men rode up and accused us of trying to steal her. It was one of theirs, but we'd worked for over an hour to get her out. And I'd bet ten bucks they were up on the ridge the whole damn time laughing and letting us do all the work."

"You did the right thing."

"We know that, but it was their damn attitude. I'm going to wash up. I got time?"

Glenna smiled at him. "Plenty of time. Slocum has some neat plans for those pushy rannies."

"Yeah, I'd have them crap on a bear trap—" Carter went on toward the small bunkhouse. "That would fix them."

"I guess you see he don't like them either. Who were they, Jon?" she asked.

"One guy I knew was named Rocky. The other was a new man. He never offered his name, but he's more Texas trash."

"I have fresh coffee. Let's go inside. First nice day around here. I hope there will be more."

Slocum agreed.

They talked and laughed over Slocum's plans. Jon, Carter, and Glenna were more than ready to try and rid the range of these bad-mouths that Horace Garvin had hired. Carter really liked the ideas and was ready to start putting them into action.

"We have the blasting sticks," Jon said as their conversation wound down.

The two men excused themselves and went to the bunkhouse, leaving Slocum and Glenna sitting in front of the low fire in the fireplace. It felt good because the temperature fell fast after sundown.

"Tell me all about your childhood," she said. "I bet you had an interesting life growing up."

"I was raised on a farm in south Georgia. Did all the things boys did growing up and then got caught up in the war."

"What happened after that? Did you go home and farm?"

"I did, sure. I was starting to build the family farm back up from the ruin it had become during the war. But a greedy carpetbagger judge tried to take the farm away from me. I turned he tables on him and his henchman—and then had the label 'judge killer' on my back like a bull's-eye. I ended up burning the whole place to the ground and heading west."

"From what you say, that was almost ten years ago." She shook her head.

"It has been a long time. A young man died of pneumonia, and I claimed the body was that of John Slocum and collected the federal reward at Van Buren, Arkansas. That calmed things down a lot for a while. But later at Fort Scott, Kansas, a judge's son got drunk, accused me of cheating him in a card game, and drew a gun. He ended up dead. That's when they found out that John Slocum was still alive, and that judge has now had men hounding my trail for years. Then this thing at Fort Hayes happened."

"The farther you go, the deeper it gets it sounds to me."

He agreed. The fire cracking and the warmth on his face felt good after all the cold nights he'd spent in the buffalo camp. He wondered about Murty and what she'd done with all her gold and hoped, by this time, that she was living in some nice two-story house on a side street in an Iowa farm town. He might never know where his once giggling companion was sleeping or with who.

Glenna leaned forward toward the fire and then straightened to stretch over her head. "I guess those boys left us so we could be alone?"

"They acted tired from wrestling that cow out of the mud. That's hard work."

"I know. Jon and I have done that before."

"Some folks think ranching is just riding around on horseback. You do lots of that, you do lots of the other not so nice things, like saving bogged cows and pulling calves."

She clapped him on the shoulder. "You know, don't you?"

He turned and looked at her. "I know you are a good-looking woman too."

She wet her lips. "I don't know about that. I'm getting gray in my hair and nothing I can do about that."

"Not to be nosey, but do you miss not having a husband?"

She closed her eyes. "There were times I could have killed him. He was so damn bullheaded. But then we'd have a session in bed and I'd think he was going to change. But he never did—rode off on that bronc horse I knew was going kill him, and it did."

They both stood up, and he kissed her. Soft, tender lip contact—he could feel that she was still shaking from remembering her man's past ignorance. Then her arms went around his neck and they smooched some more.

Her eyes closed as she sought more from his mouth. Then, finally out of breath, she twisted her face away. "I feel like a silly teenage girl. He never kissed me like that, and I'll be honest, you have me shaking again."

"If it bothers you, I'll quit."

She shook her hair back. "No, I have an edge inside of me, to always get closer to a cliff and see over to the bottom. You are that cliff edge."

"What next?"

"Well, it will be your choice. Go get your bedroll and put it on the floor. I can always say you slept on the floor."

"Fine."

"Meanwhile, I will get out of my clothes. Would you wear a dead man's nightshirt? That's a pretty strange question to ask, isn't it?" She laughed, but it was more of a strained laugh than anything funny.

He brought his bedroll inside, unstrapped it, and rolled it out in the fire's light on the floor. Then he saw the nightshirt on the back of the chair. She was serious. He unbuckled his gun belt, hung it on the chair, then removed his boots, and next his pants, and then his vest and shirt. His looming shadow from the fireplace's light on the room's wall was one of a giant getting into the nightshirt.

Where was she at? In the bedroom, off the kitchen, he

guessed. The floor was smooth and clean under his bare soles. From the doorway he could see the metal four-poster bed frame, and he went to the right side, which was vacant, and pulled the cover back to crawl in. He noted the satin-covered down-filled comforter on top when he lay on his side and looked at the form of her back.

"Have you changed your mind?" he asked.

"No."

"Good."

"Why?"

"Because you're a beautiful woman and I want to have you."

"I knew that. I read it in your eyes when I first saw you. I couldn't believe how restrained you were toward me all afternoon."

"It had to be two-way street for me to participate."

"Nice, but it put me on edge. Not that one but a nervous one. *Would I please him?*"

"Why wouldn't you?"

"You kissed me. Granger never did. He was the only man I have ever known as a mate. I must have pleased him, since he never complained about that part of our life, but he never said good, bad, or terrible when he was through. But you have drawn things in my mind that I never felt before. Oh, my first night with Granger I shook some, but when it was over I felt relaxed, and I looked forward to the end of the next time bringing me that settled feeling again. We did it a lot when we first were married, then it got to be routine and further apart. I expected to become pregnant, but in three years I never did. So I guessed it would not happen."

"I have no idea how it will begin or end, but I hope we both enjoy it."

She scooted closer. "I had to have these nightclothes to start. Forgive me?"

"I do," he said and pulled her toward him to kiss. After a few minutes, he tugged on her nightgown bottom and she raised her butt for him to gather it up.

In minutes he was kissing her breasts, making her nipples rock-hard, and she moaned under his attention.

"Let me get out of this thing." She huffed and sat up to tear it off over her head and toss it aside. Then she grabbed Slocum's nightshirt impatiently, as if she meant to rip it off of him.

"Easy now," he said and eased her hand back. Then in one swift motion he lifted the shirt up over his head and off, and she fell back in his arms.

"Oh, I am enjoying your attention so much," she said.

"So am I. So am I."

His finger began to probe her gently, drawing the lubricant into her channel. When he thought she was ready, he moved between her knees and started inside her.

"He's big," she whispered, but her passageway enlarged to fit him. Then he pushed through her ring and she gasped, hugging him. "Don't quit. I'm fine."

Their actions were wild and the ropes creaked. Her bare heels beat on his legs, and they went on and on. When it was over, they fell asleep in each other's arms.

Sometime in the night they awoke and had another session, and then later she woke him in a state of alarm. "Go sleep in your bedroll. They will be here in a short while. I'll dress and help you."

She quickly dressed and smoothed her clothes out. Then she brushed her hair fierce-like. "Do I show anywhere what we did?"

He laughed. "Did you relax any?"

"Oh my God. Did I ever relax. Oh—" She put her forearm to her forehead. "Yes, I really did relax." Then she kissed him and hurried away.

He dressed in the front room after stoking the fireplace.

More cold weather was on its way. His back felt stiff. Not from their efforts, but his back muscles contracted at the approach of a storm. Winter wasn't over yet.

"I have you a cup of coffee poured," she said after he finished rolling up his bedroll.

"Coming." He slipped onto a chair at the table. "Sleep all right?"

"Never any better, how about you?"

"After the first or second time?" he asked.

"Both."

"Oh, I could do it again."

"Well we will have to see about that, Mr. Slocum."

The others were coming. He heard them on the porch shuffling in.

"You two sleep last night?" Jon asked.

"Sure. He slept on the floor in his bedroll and me in my own bed. Why?"

"Aw, we heard lots of screeching and yelling going on over here. Thought you two were fighting."

Hands on her hips, she scowled at her brother. "Jon."

"Aw, hell, I was just funning. I'm glad he came by, and he can sleep on your floor any night."

"Slocum, do you see what I must put up with?" she asked him.

"I do."

"Well what do we do today?" Jon asked

"We are making a dummy to hang and several chains of tin cans to tie on their horses' tails and getting otherwise ready to run that mouthy bunch out of Nebraska."

"Amen," Carter said. "I'm going to be a little mouse too and watch that come off."

"Let's do it," Glenna said and smiled at them, holding pancakes and fried eggs on platters.

"You bet," Jon said. "Slocum, I have had a belly full of that Texas trash."

"Better eat your breakfast, boys. You're going to be real busy today."

Good, Slocum thought as he passed the plate of eggs. He'd talk to Jon today about buying a horse too.

10

The stuffed dummy took shape easily. Glenna made a head and face on the pillowcase and they sewed an old hat on it. Carter built the hangman's noose and that was applied to the dummy's neck and stitched on too so it didn't pull the head off when they hung the whole thing up.

Slocum punched holes in rusty tin cans with a punch and hammer in the blacksmith shop they had. The others tied them on long strings, separated so they'd make lots of noise when the horses started off from the hitch rack. Each chain was placed in an individual gunnysack so they didn't get tangled up. Then Jon, Carter, and Slocum sharpened their jackknives so they would be sharp enough to cut through the cinches on the horses.

Before dark the three men rode into Buttercup and hitched their horses out back. It was no trouble staying hidden in the darkness out front of the noisy saloon.

Hitching the strings to the ponies' tails proved harder than expected, so they tied part of them to the back girths. But everything was finally set, and all they had to do was wait. Carter was posted between the saddle shop and the mercantile. Slocum and Jon were upstairs of what at one time had been the local cathouse, before the madam moved on to richer fields to plow with her girls. The place was now empty, and they had ringside seats at the open windows for the fandango they expected to happen about midnight. The weather still was mild. They talked in low voices, spending the time talking about some good horses they'd owned.

A drunk staggered out of the batwing doors. Slocum watched him close as he went to a Garvin horse, but he was too drunk to get on him. So he went back and lay down to sleep on the porch. With a shake of his head over how close they'd come to losing the trick, Slocum shared a look with Jon. Damn that had been close.

It was closing time and the ranch hands began to wander outside. A big man stretched. "Let's get home, guys. Toss Fenell over his horse. He's too drunk to ride."

Two guys draped the drunk over his saddle and used his rope to tie him on. One guy got in his saddle. His cinch broke and turned him upside down. Another horse jerked and cans rattled. Cowboys cussed. Another bronc stuck his head to the ground and dumped the rider off. The cans had spooked all the horses, who climbed over one another trying to escape, clanging away, cinches breaking. Stomping on their boot soles and cussing, cowboys tried to separate the saddled horses from the saddle-less ones. Several mounts ran away from the town with tin cans chasing them.

Someone shouted, "If I ever catch the goddamn sumbitch did this to us, he's dead. I mean a dead ass."

"Damn right, Logan. We'll help you kill him."

"We better get to hiking, boys. We ain't got a damn horse left here to ride."

"Ah, shit, who did this?"

"We'll find them. If it takes all I've got. We'll find them."

"We've got us some real enemies, boys. Wait till the old man hears about it."

The Garvin ranch hands started to walk home. Slocum shook Jon's hand, and they sat back to wait until the other men were well gone.

"By grab, that was the best show I ever watched," Carter said when they mounted up to ride home. "That outfit should know now we mean business."

"They'll learn," Slocum agreed. "Dummy hangs next."

"What then?" Jon asked.

"Use a candle deal and blow up the corral fencing and scatter their remuda all over hell."

"We may have to wait until after the rain. I figure it's moving in," Jon said, looking at the cloud cover dimming the night.

"No problem. They need to think about this past night. And then we get to remind them, again, that they need to leave." Slocum was also busy figuring other things to spring on them.

"Do those cowboys sleep out much?" he asked.

"I guess," Carter said.

"Then we need to slip notes in their bedrolls to get out."

"That may be hard."

"We'll see. We need to be ready for the chance."

Both men agreed with him. They arrived back at the ranch, and Glenna got up to welcome them. "I have warm soup and fresh sourdough bread. Come in and eat. You all must be starved. I want to hear what happened."

They trooped inside, dead tired, and sat at the table eating her food.

"How did it go?" she asked.

Carter looked up from a large spoonful of beef chunks that he was getting ready to put in his mouth. "Girl, it was wonderful. A dang drunk stumbled outside. I thought he'd ruin it all, but he went back when he couldn't get on his horse. When they all came out, they loaded him on his horse and tied him down. Then a horse spooked and dragged a chain of cans. More cans rattled, and so some of the horses bucked; cinches broke and cowboys were spilled all over the street. There was so much going on so fast you couldn't see it all happening."

"Then they walked home," Slocum added. "But they will be on their guard. And they were mad as hornets."

"So are lots of us who have felt their edge. We got in a good jab. Go to sleep. It is Sunday and I am going to church today." She gathered their bowls.

"I'll go with you," Slocum said. "We have no idea how they will react to this treatment."

"That's fine. But I can handle it myself."

"I'll go with you." He wasn't going to let her slough him off. There was no telling what the ranch hands' response to the past night would be, and he didn't want her hurt.

"All right, you can go with me. But you can't sleep in church."

They all laughed. The other two men went to the bunkhouse. He started for his bedroll and she took him to her bed, pulled off his boots, and told him to get undressed and get some sleep.

He did not argue. She leaned over and kissed him. "Go to sleep."

"Yes ma'am." In minutes, he was sound asleep, and he only partially knew when she joined him, but he recalled that before falling off again, he smiled to himself, when she crowded up against his back and threw her arm over him.

He drove the buckboard and wore a white shirt that belonged to Jon. It was warm and cloudy. They took slickers, and Slocum put a Winchester in the scabbard on the dashboard.

Glenna wore a starched blue dress and a scarf over her

head and shoulders. She looked very pretty, straight-backed seated beside him. The matched light team stepped out smartly. They made the trip quickly to the schoolhouse, and he helped her down then parked the team while she visited with friends in the bright sun. Jon's rain warning had evaporated, with a strong south wind no doubt pushing the clouds away.

He joined her and she introduced him as John Clark.

"Nice to meet you, John," a gray-headed lady said.

He nodded, then they made their way inside. They sat on benches toward the back. Many families were there, and they sang hymns and prayed, and the minister read something from John and preached on the subject.

There was some social gathering outside after, and Slocum met other ranchers, who had a few curious questions to ask him.

"You know about Garvin's efforts to run us all off?" one man asked.

"Yes, Glenna told me all about it. You may need to organize and meet him head-on."

"Aw, few of us are tough enough to meet them gunhands of his like that."

"They force you far enough back, you may need to do that."

"I sure dread the whole thing."

Slocum agreed. Glenna nodded that she was ready to go, and she said good-bye to everyone. They walked to where the buckboard team was tied to a hitch post. He untied the horses, straightened the lines, and handed them to her before he climbed up and joined her.

"Thanks," she said, squeezing his arm when he sat beside her.

"Clark?"

"I didn't want you exposed. All I could think of in such a short time."

"No problem. Good thinking." He clucked to the horses, and they swept away for the ranch.

They topped a rolling hill, and he saw half a dozen riders in the road. Two or three had their arms in slings or their heads bandaged.

He wanted to laugh, but instead he said, "Get the rifle out and then take the reins."

She did. "That's Sears. Watch him."

"I will."

The horses sawed down to a walk, and he handed her the reins. He reached for and loaded the rifle with the lever, cocked it, and balanced the rifle butt on his knee.

"What do you think?" she asked under her breath when the riders held their place in the road.

"Stop the horses."

"Who the hell are you?" the man she called Sears asked him from under his droopy-brim brown felt hat.

"The man that's going to blow your brains out if you don't get out of the road."

Sears checked his horse. "You talk damn tough for a man outgunned here."

"You won't know if I am or I'm not, because you'll die first." Slocum rose and took aim at him.

"Someone messed with our horses last night in town. You know anything about it?"

"I know you're blocking a public road. Get the hell aside or you will die." He held the gun pointed at the big man's heart.

"I asked you a question."

"Move or die!"

"Hold it. We are going to find out who messed with our horses, and when we do, we'll hang them."

The rifle still nested in his shoulder, Slocum motioned with the barrel for Sears to move aside. When he looked at the rest of the riders, Slocum saw that only a few of the enemy looked gun-ready enough to fight him.

Glenna drove the horses through them and they hurried for the ranch. He left the rifle on safety, and in the exchange with her, he took the reins and she put the gun away, looking back at their dust wake. "They aren't coming. My, my, you all sure battered them up. I had no idea they would be that broken up."

"The plan worked much better than I'd even dreamed. Four of those guys couldn't use a gun, did you notice?"

"So you had only two shooters to face?"

When she squeezed his arm, he leaned over and smiled. "They are not in great shape. We need to close in on them.

"Back there you looked pretty gutsy to me for you to take a stand with a rifle against six men."

"I wanted them to think they weren't in shape to run things. Next I want to scatter their remuda and make that tough on them."

"You did have an upper hand looking at all those bandaged men he had to ride with him."

"That's his foreman?"

"Yes, that's Sears. I am surprised the old man wasn't with them. Garvin's a tough old buzzard too."

"What the hell was Sears looking for out here?" Slocum shook his head. "They might have split up hoping to find the villains who did that to them."

She laughed. "Who would tell them anyway?"

"They felt after our attack caught them off guard, they needed to flex their muscles or lose their hold."

"That battered up bunch couldn't whip much." She shook her head and squeezed his arm.

"They still have to keep up their faces, but word will get out that someone outfoxed them and that they are in too poor a condition to enforce much right now."

"I hope they all flee." She leaned against his shoulder, then grinned.

That evening, after midnight, Slocum and Jon installed the dummy on the Garvin ranch crossbar. Jon stood on his saddle to tie it into place. Slocum felt wary the entire time, thinking that being only such a short distance from the ranch headquarters, they might be discovered. He held Jon's horse to steady him while Jon finished with the knots.

Finally, Jon dropped down into the saddle and took the reins up in the starlight. "He's secure. Let's go."

"Right."

"I wish I could see their faces when they find him tomorrow."

Slocum agreed, then looked back at the dark buildings. *Well, Garvin, round two and we will win again.*

On a grassy ridge under a sliver of a moon, they cut the gunnysacks off their horses' feet. The effort had been to make it harder to follow their tracks. They wadded up the gunnysacks, tied them on their saddles, so they left no evidence, and rode for home.

"When do we blow up the corrals?" Jon asked.

"Oh, in another week. By then they will have relaxed again, and will have started asking, 'What else could they do to us?' "

"I savvy. Shame we couldn't watch them discover the dummy."

"Ah, better yet for us to see their horses' butts go over the hill for Texas or some other parts."

"I hope to see that too."

"Yes. I'm taking Glenna to Buttercup for supplies today. We better get back so I can sleep a few hours."

"I gotta hand it to you. She's a damn sight easier to live with since you came around," Jon said and looked off into the night.

"What was he like?"

"Her husband was a tough guy. He'd been raised tough somewhere. He had little patience with anyone. He riled me up a time or two. We had a few fistfights, but we got to where we got along. Still, he was like a bulldog around her. He growled a lot and that made me mad, but she said she could defend herself."

"You ever see him kiss her?"

"No, why?"

"She told me that and I could hardly believe her."

Jon shook his head. "You never knew Russell."

"I think I do now."

"I felt the same way." Talking about him was over.

They got back, put their horses up, and Slocum split with Jon and went into the dark house. Inside, she must have heard him, and she lit a lamp in the bedroom.

He stood in the doorway and admired her in the light and her nightgown. She fussed with her hair, coming across the room. His arms around her, he hugged and kissed her hard, and she sighed, "Whew."

"The dummy's been hung."

She pressed her belly harder to him. "Sounds wonderful."

He agreed and kissed her again.

As if he had never kissed her—

11

Slocum hitched the team after breakfast, and they left for town. The drive was a two-hour trip one way. A few clouds were gathering, and they could sure use the rain. Things were dry for springtime. They'd planted her potatoes, cabbage, and carrots. Glenna wanted different seed for later plantings, flour, baking powder, sugar . . . her list went on.

They were making good time when he spotted the dust coming from the west. Someone was coming or several someones were coming toward the main road. They'd soon meet them.

"Horses and riders," she said and reached for the Winchester.

He agreed, keeping an eye on them as they drew up in the road. A shift of wind exposed them. It was Sears, three men, and an older man on a big black stud horse.

When he reined up, Sears booted his horse over toward them. "Well, rifleman, we meet again. He your new husband, Glenna?"

"Wouldn't be none of your business anyway," she said, scowling at him.

"What are you up to, Sears?" Slocum asked him. "You sure aren't working cattle, are you? Scaring more homesteaders away?"

"You better mind your own business, stranger. You might get a bullet between your eyes."

"Draw then. This .44/40 might improve your manners."

"Just who the hell are you?" Garvin demanded and started his horse toward them.

"Stay there, mister. I think Sears wants to toss in his chips here." His hand used the rifle barrel to direct Garvin to back up.

"Shoot him," Garvin said.

Sears took a hard look at Slocum, shook his head, and turned his horse away. "Shoot him yourself. That sumbitch will kill you."

Slocum's attention shifted, and the rifle centered on the older man. "It's a good day to die."

Garvin shook his head, tried to cover his red-faced anger, and reined his horse back to the others. "My day will come."

"Wear a good suit of clothes that day," Slocum said. "Drive on, Glenna."

The sullen riders sat on their horses as the old man, with his hands on his saddle horn, steamed. Two of the men still had their arms in slings.

Slocum stood up, his legs braced, as she swept the rig around them, and he held the Winchester ready to answer to anyone who wanted to be shot. They soon were away from Garvin and his men, and he put the rifle on safety.

"I'm sorry they are so hard to live with."

"Not your fault." She reined the team down to a trot. "I'm just proud you were along. Saved me killing two or three of them myself."

He took the reins back and laughed. "Yes. You might have done that."

They shopped in town, loaded the buckboard with their

supplies, ate lunch in the small café, and then she went to see about buying a church dress at the seamstress shop while he bought some leather for saddle repairs.

"You're new here, ain'tcha?" the saddle-maker asked him.

"Yes. I'm helping Mrs. Russell and Jon out at their place."

"Nice lady. My name's Earl Stokes. Give her my regards. Guess you heard about the big blowup the Double G Bar bunch had here last Saturday night?"

Slocum shook his head.

"Well that bunch is rowdy and bossy as hell. They all came in to drink and take over the saloon. But when they came out about midnight, someone had tied tin cans to their horses' tails and, they say, cut their cinches. About bought out all my cinches. I have more coming, but it will be a few weeks. They got all busted up and are offering a hundred-dollar reward for whoever did it."

"Sounds serious."

"Broken arms and legs and busted heads. They sure had hell."

"Reckon they've got enemies?"

"Oh, they run roughshod over everyone. Old man wants to run off everyone and have the range to himself. I never caught your name?"

"Clark," he said and shook the man's hand.

"Staying long?"

"Long enough." Slocum picked up the rolled-up hide.

"Tell them two hello for me."

"I will." He left the shop and put the hide in the loaded buckboard. Glenna soon joined him and asked if he'd met the saddle maker.

"Nice guy. He told me all about the wreck those boys had Saturday night here."

"They told me about it in the dress shop too." He helped her onto the spring seat, then joined her and untied the reins.

"Guess they really want the ones who did that to them."

"Marie in there said three had already quit over the fracas and others were going to leave when they got healed."

"It's working." He clucked to the team and then started the drive out of town.

She agreed with a nod, and when they were beyond prying eyes on the prairie, she hugged his arm and bumped his shoulder with hers. "Anything to get rid of that nuisance makes me happy. I wish you could stay forever, but there is no way I know to permanently hide you."

"Right. But for now, I enjoy your company and your generosity toward me."

"Hey, my life was pretty dull until you came along."

"The saddle maker ever court you?"

"No. You mean Stokes?"

"He sounded like you were a favorite of his."

"Really?"

"Yes."

"Another day, another time, maybe."

"Hey, if I am in the way—"

"You damn sure are not in the way of anything."

"Yes, ma'am."

"What do we do next?"

"Blow up a corral and scatter his horses."

"How hard is that?"

"We have to sneak in when they aren't looking, use the candle fuse and strap all the blasting sticks to posts, and get set for a big blowup. The horses will panic, and with the corral down, they will run away I hope."

"Sounds good."

"We might set another at the bunkhouse if we have time to do it."

Jon and Carter checked on the cattle and at night made cedar shavings. Slocum tested two of the tubes to be certain the fuses ignited. One took an hour and a half, the other one required near two hours, but they both ignited in the end. He knew his plan would work. Next came the final part. Cutting the blasting sticks in two, arming them, and crimping the cord on the firing tube. They had lots of strong plain cord and cut it in lengths to go around the posts to hold the blasting sticks in place.

They left their horses in a draw nearly a quarter mile away from the ranch headquarters. Glenna insisted on coming along and holding the horses.

"No matter what happens, you stay here. Things get hot, you ride like hell for home," Slocum said.

"Yes, yes," she agreed.

They hung their spurs on their saddle horns. With the stealth of Indians they came up out of the willows and approached the corrals from the backside. The night guard's whistling to stay awake warned them. He was somewhere near the pens. Slocum told Jon and Carter to stay there and to listen for two owl hoots before they came in. He had managed to get along the fence when some sleeping horses had a kicking fit and distracted the lookout.

When the man stepped off the fence, after ordering the horses apart, which made little difference, Slocum conked him on the head. He crumpled to the ground. Slocum hooted twice and then quickly gagged the guard with his kerchief. By then Jon and Carter were there and they tied the man up.

"What do we do with him?" Jon whispered.

"Leave him for now, but we will take him with us if we have to." They nodded and set to work.

Things went swiftly, and soon the entire setup was in place and ready. Carter even got one tube set up underneath the bunkhouse.

The man was still groggy, so Jon and Carter carried him along blindfolded. Slocum carried the man's rifle. On the way he whispered in Jon's ear not to talk and to warn Glenna as well. Carter heard and agreed with a nod in the starlight.

"Who—" she started, but Jon silenced her.

The man was moaning. Slocum whispered in his ear to shut up or he'd cut his throat. That silenced him. They carried him south along the creek that fed Garvin's ranch from north to south. Then they left him barefooted, tied to a tree, blinded and gagged.

"One word from you about who we are and you are a dead goose. Savvy?" Slocum asked.

The man, obviously shaken, nodded.

They rode off for home, on a roundabout course, leaving fewer hoofprints by riding down the creek rather than in the grass. Near two o'clock they were home and put up their horses. After all that, they couldn't wait to hear what destruction they'd done. It began to rain a few hours later, which, Slocum realized while in bed with her, was the best trail washing he could have planned on. Hugging her from behind, he went back to sleep.

Garvin's men should have the clue after this deal: *It was leave or die.*

12

A deputy sheriff showed up at the ranch two days later asking questions. His name was Kenyon Welles. He was a short man in his thirties who rode a plain bay horse and looked like a cowboy.

Jon knew him and introduced Slocum as John Clark. "Nice to meet you, sir," the sheriff said.

He removed his hat when Glenna came to the door. "Nice to see you, Mrs. Russell. Got a question or two to ask. Night before last someone or several someones blew up the Two G Bar ranch's corral and scattered their remuda to the winds. Of course it rained that night with thunder and lightning, and that drove the horses even further away.

"They say they had a guard out there and that the raiders must have killed him, but I got reliable word that he ran off after the deal and jumped a freight train that next night. They also blew one charge off under the bunkhouse, which hurt about three men seriously when they were thrown out of their bunks. Someone wanted them gone. You four have any idea who could have done that?"

112

"No idea. Does Garvin have any help left?" Glenna asked.

"Not many. Several quit and left like that guard did. I don't blame them, but one of them said someone even hung a dummy up at the crossbar and it had a sign on it telling them to leave. They are like rats jumping from a sinking ship. You don't know anyone hated him that much?"

"We all hate him. Every small rancher and homesteader hates Garvin and his crew's high-handed ways, but as to who did it that's your guess," Glenna said.

"Mrs. Russell, I have that impression from talking to folks. These men don't have many folks like them. But it still is breaking the law to blow up someone's property and injure folks, and it is my job to find the offenders. They also claimed some parties, earlier, tied tin cans on their horses' tails and cut cinches when they were in town. That caused them a whole bunch of injuries."

"We know you are doing your job, Kenyon, but Garvin has pushed and threatened everyone in this country. I'd say I'm grateful to whoever did it. You find him and I'll start a fund to get him off," Glenna said.

"Just remember, I am only doing my job."

Jon nodded. "We know that. Thanks for coming by."

"Good day, ma'am, and the rest of you. Nice to meet you too, Clark." He rode off.

When he was gone, Carter slapped his knee. "That ole night guard hopped a freight train and was gone. Kenyon learned that much anyway. We put the fear of God in him all right. I bet he was still barefooted."

"Probably. I bet they're six months getting their horses back with whatever help he does have left," Glenna said and took a hard look in the direction the deputy rode off in. "And they won't find them all."

"Right," Slocum said. "Do I smell lunch?"

"You do. Wash up, killers." Then she laughed.

That night in bed, the two of them were still talking about their results.

The consensus in town was that Garvin was down to four men who could even ride horses, and they weren't finding them very fast. The estimate was that he was over a hundred head short.

A hand who worked in the livery told Slocum, while he waited on Glenna to get her new dress fitted, that all they had to ride were the old horses they could catch on foot. He chuckled and said, "Three of them went through here a day ago. They'd been in that bunkhouse when it blew up, and so they up and quit. They couldn't hear jack shit. I had to shout at them to even talk. I think it will be Garvin and Sears as the only ones left to find them horses."

"They can't do much good."

"Garvin's too tight to hire some local boys around here to go look for them horses."

"Good enough for him."

"I think he's close to selling out."

"You hear that for a fact?"

"No, but he better. That outfit that's after him will blow him up next."

Slocum agreed. He saw that Glenna had come out of the dress shop. "Thanks. You hear he wants to sell, send me word."

"I sure will, Mr. Clark."

He left the man leaning on his pitchfork and assisted Glenna onto the loaded buckboard, then went around, climbed on himself, and took up the reins.

"You get the dress?"

"They still need to make some stitches. It will be ready next time we come to town."

"Sounds good. Anything else?"

"Three more of his men quit who lost their hearing."

"I learned that too. But they were warned. The swamper at the livery thinks he's down to just him and Sears."

"They are not finding the horses very fast either."

"That many horses, and they'll only get wilder the longer they are free."

"You're right."

Slocum clucked to speed up the team, and the warmer day felt good. He needed one more good plan to push Garvin over. He was teetering on the brink; all he'd needed was a shove.

When they dropped into the cottonwoods and willows along the creek, a shot rang out. Slocum charged the horses to get the hell out of the dense, head-high brush beside the road, wondering where the shooter was at.

"I don't see anyone. Keep going," Glenna said, drawing his six-gun out of his holster between them. "I'm fine, but I still can't see him."

"There he is," she said. The pistol roared, and he could smell the gun smoke as he held down the spooked team.

"Get him?"

"I got his horse. Guess I was shooting too low. What should we do?"

"Get our butts home. No telling how many there are of them. You know who it was?"

"Sears. I'd know him anywhere. I didn't mean to shoot his horse."

"You couldn't help about shooting the horse. I'll get myself a horse and come back. Remind me to reload my Colt when we get to the ranch. And my answer is no, you don't need to come back. Too dangerous."

"I'm not afraid."

"I know you aren't, but I may have enough trouble for myself."

"I won't be a problem to you."

"Glenna, stay at the ranch."

"And wring my hands?"

"Yes."

"Well, isn't that a fine kettle of fish to stew over."

"I know nothing about stewing fish. But one person is enough to worry about in this case. That's me."

"I could choke you. I want to go along and help."

"I don't need help. Do you understand?"

"You will. And you will rue the day you left me behind."

"Glenna, I don't want you hurt."

"Oh. You are like all men. You think I'm some sissy and can't help."

"I know you are capable enough. But two people is one too many to worry about chasing down a bastard like Sears."

"What will I tell Jon and Carter when they come in?"

"That I went to find him. And I'll be back."

"They'll want to find you."

"Tell them where I went then."

"Why not leave them a note?"

"Glenna."

"I know you don't want to have to worry about me. Slocum-Clark, you are the most stubborn man I have ever met." She clapped her hands on her legs.

He swung the rig into the yard, making a cloud of dust, and headed it for the corral. She gripped the seat bottom on both sides hard so as not to sway much, but they both did, and he hauled them down near the corral.

"I can unharness them. Go get a horse. I'll send Jon and Carter to help you when they come in. How will you mark the trail?"

"Break limbs off as I go."

He was soon inside the corral, building a loop in the riata. The horses were spooked and moved down-pen to escape him.

"Take the bay horse they call Spook, Slocum. He's an old stud horse that they caught running with a band of mares. He's tough but will sure get you there." Glenna's knees were against the second rail from the top to help balance her standing, and she held the tall corral post to observe his actions.

His first throw missed, and Spook really shied when he realized this man wanted him. Busy reeling in the riata, Slocum moved to head him off. The next loop whirled over the horse's head as he ran by at full steam. The noose went over Spook's ears, and Slocum set his boot heels in to stop him. He wondered for a moment if the horse would drag him, but Spook stopped, trembling all over as Slocum approached him and coiled rope at the same time. He made a halter and led the horse to the barn. The blood bay blew boogers out the end of nose and nickered a lot to Slocum. Slocum spoke to him in soft words to reassure him and settle him down. The lariat hitched to an iron ring, he brought out his blankets and saddle. When they were tossed on Spook's back, Slocum talking the whole time, he drew up the girth and the big horse shied, but not much. Glenna was at the gate, holding his rifle from the buckboard.

"You have ammunition for this rifle?" she asked.

He nodded, more intent on how the bull-necked horse would act when he finished saddling him and had the bit in his mouth

"What about food?" she asked. "I have some jerky we can put in your saddlebags."

"Sure." The horse circled away from him at the sight of the rifle, like it might be a club. Slocum caught up with him and jammed the gun in the scabbard. Then he pulled the horse up closer. Glenna ran for her jerky, disappearing through the back door. Slocum mused at the showing of her white legs with the dress hem raised to free her to run. No need to mount the horse until he had the food loaded—he wasn't called Spook because he was a sleeper, Slocum knew that.

She had the jerky wrapped in meat paper and stuck it in the saddlebags. "Don't let them shoot you."

He kissed her and with one arm hugged her. "Thanks. You're great."

She chewed on her lower lip. "Get the hell out of here."

"You be careful and have a gun handy. No telling whether they may be real desperate by now." He grasped the headstall in his left hand and cranked the horse's head around against his left leg. That made him spin around, but he couldn't buck if he was spinning.

At last seated in the saddle, with his boots in the stirrups, he shouted, "Hee-yah!" in the bay's ear. The spurs gouging his sides confused Spook's mind enough to make him charge out of the yard, and Slocum turned him northbound on the road. They left in a fury of flying hooves and dust. Spook never had a chance to buck, and Slocum was on his way back to the horse Glenna had shot in the road.

A short while later, he reined up short of the obviously dead animal. Still tense, Spook shuffled sideways. Buzzards that had been on the ground, surveying their next meal, had taken wing at their approach, which made the horse shy at their flapping wings. Sears's saddle was still on the horse, pinned under the dead piebald's body.

Dismounted, Slocum searched around the place for signs of boot tracks. They were there, and obviously he'd come back after they left to try and recover his saddle. No way he could do that, and even his Winchester was pinned under the body. No way to get it out either. So Sears's only gun now was no doubt a pistol. That was good news. And he was on foot, unless he came with someone, and there were no signs of that. Once he left this brushy site on the creek, he'd be out in the sea of Nebraska grass and should be easy to find. Slocum sent Spook for the high point on the hill so he could scope the country that lay west—in the direction of the ranch—to see if he could spot Sears. The horse was powerful. He cat hopped up the steep slope and soon stopped on the highest point. With the field glasses from his saddlebags, Slocum viewed the country for sight of Sears's hat. Lots of swaying grass moving like an ocean in the wind— where in the hell had he gone?

No sight of him. The prairie had gobbled him whole, Slocum mused. It had taken over two hours for Slocum to get back to the ranch and then return to the scene of the attack. No telling how far Sears had gone. Slocum set off from the hilltop and planned to ride farther west and look more for any sight of the man.

In another hour, he spotted smoke and headed toward it. Maybe he should have brought Glenna along. At least he'd have had company to share this empty country with. Then he spotted the soddy and the area cleared for a garden. There were some corrals, chickens, and wash flapping on the clothes-lines.

He used the glasses to scan some more. No one was in sight, nor did anyone move. Then he centered his vision on the body of a dog close by the door. Fresh blood shone where his head had been caved in. Why kill a dog at your doorstep? Nothing else around that place was that far out of being perfect. He replaced the field glasses in his saddlebags.

Rifle across his lap, he approached the home place—real wary. He dismounted—the silence, save for the busy chickens scratching and clucking in their own world didn't concern him. Where were the residents?

Smoke came from a cookstove. He could smell the flavor of it. Too warm to need heat. He slipped into the house and let his eyes adjust to the shadowy interior.

A wide-eyed woman, gagged and naked, was tied on the top of the bed. He set the rifle down and drew the knife from his belt. The woman fainted. Swiftly, in a few seconds, he cut the ropes and then took the gag off her face.

She rolled over on her side in a fetal crouch to hide her nakedness and moaned.

"Lady, I'm sorry." He tossed her a wash-worn dress and turned his back. "Who did this to you?"

"Garvin's foreman—Sears. He also stole a horse. I heard him ride off on one of them. Thank God you came. I might have died tied here."

"How long ago was he here?"

"I don't know. It was like an eternity laying there tied up." She straightened out the dress she'd put on. "My name's Helen Gladdis."

"Slocum's mine. I'm looking for that same man. He shot at me this morning."

"Sears?"

He nodded.

"He was alone this time—"

Slocum narrowed his gaze at her. "He's been here before?"

"Sure. A widow woman is helpless to defend herself against the likes of him and that scum that runs with him."

"You tell the sheriff?"

She shook her head. "Why? It would have been my word against him and his men."

A woman in her late twenties–early thirties, she was plain-looking and thin. No doubt rock-hard from doing her own chores, but hardly a handsome woman. Her brown hair she had put back in a bun behind her head.

"Excuse my bad manners. I'll make you some coffee." She paused. "Do you drink it?"

He laughed. No doubt she wondered if he was a Mormon. "Yes, I'd like a cup."

"All right. Do you live around here?"

He shook his head. "I've been staying at the Russell ranch and helping them."

"She is a very pretty woman."

He agreed. "How do you make it?"

"I own a hundred cows that are marked with my brand,

the Key Brand. I hire day help at roundup and I make enough sales to survive."

"What happened to your husband?"

"Oh, he took a fever one day and got sicker and sicker. I went and got a doctor. He didn't know a thing he could do, and a week later my husband died."

"How long ago?"

"Three years."

"No, suitors?"

"I'm too fussy and not that pretty, but Sears won't rape me again. I got my back up. I'll kill him next time."

"I'll bury your dog."

"No, I'll do it in the morning. Must be close to supper-time."

Slocum heard riders and knew when Spook nickered at the horses that it was Jon and Carter. He went to the door as they arrived on lathered horses.

"You find him?" Jon called as they pulled up.

"I'll be back," he said over his shoulder to the woman and went to meet the men in the yard.

"He was here earlier," Slocum said under his breath. "Raped her and stole a horse. She's pretty upset, so go easy on her."

"What killed the dog?" Carter asked.

"Sears."

Carter scowled. "He raped her?"

Slocum nodded. "Left her tied, gagged, and naked on the bed."

Carter glared at the house. "That sumbitch needs to be shot."

"I agree, but he had ridden off on one of her horses by the time I got here."

"She's a tough woman," Jon said under his breath. "I don't know how she's survived out here—alone."

"It wasn't his first time to rape her either."

"Ah shit, let's find him." Carter was madder than a wet rooster.

Helen came to the door. "I have enough food if you'd like to stay. Thanks for coming by."

"You two know Helen?" Slocum asked

"We do. Good to see you, ma'am."

She made a pleased face at them. "Wash up. There will be enough time to unsaddle and put them in the corral."

Carter shook his head. "I'll wring his neck if we catch him."

"I agree," Jon said.

"Both of you sure that Glenna is all right?" Slocum asked.

Jon laughed, hoisting off his saddle. "Besides being mad 'cause you made her stay home, she'll be fine."

"I figure Sears made a beeline on her horse to Garvin's outfit."

"That's still four hours west."

"There will be a moon tonight. Let's be there when the sun comes up. I'd like to catch them asleep."

"We can do that," Jon said.

Carter agreed.

She fixed them some fried ham, potatoes, and biscuits with gravy. Carter looked interested in her and shared some small conversation with her. She answered him like she was flattered. Slocum busied himself eating her good food.

"We must leave here about midnight to reach Garvin's by sunup," Slocum said.

"I will fix you food before you leave."

"We'd make it, but thanks."

"Hey, I count myself lucky to have three such serious men in my house."

"We wish we'd been here sooner," Carter said, cutting the biscuit floating in flour gravy with his fork. "It won't go unattended, ma'am."

She nodded, took her napkin out of her lap, and went for the coffeepot to refill their cups. Slocum thought she was about to cry, but she held it back and filled the men's cups. She was a tough woman with many struggles in her life. He felt for her.

She woke them before midnight and served a large breakfast, which included eggs, ham, and more biscuits with gravy, plus coffee. They thanked her and saddled up under her lantern light at the corral. Slocum hugged her shoulder. "We will get him."

"Thank God." She nodded and thanked them.

Carter was the last one to pass her on horseback. "God bless you, Helen."

"You too, Carter."

They rode for hours under the stars and across the rolling grass, until they reached an overlook and were able to see the dark shadows of Garvin's ranch headquarters sprawled under them. They dismounted, hung up their spurs, and hobbled their horses over the hill.

Then, on foot, they headed for the ranch, slipping off the hillside to come out behind the corral that had been repaired some since the explosions. Some poles had been tied on temporary frames to replace the old ones blown away. There were only a few horses in the corral. The three men slipped over to the remains of the bunkhouse. No one was in there.

Where they sleeping in the old man's house? Slocum, Jon, and Carter had a short conversation and decided they'd check it out. Slocum went ahead. He eased the door open, six-gun in his fist, and slipped inside. The starlight came in the windows, and he listened for someone snoring.

Only one person was in the house. He was in a side bedroom. Carter stayed outside to cover things. Jon soon joined Slocum in the house. Slocum pointed at the adjoining room and nodded.

They crept across the floor. The starlight shone down on the snoring old man in the bed. It was Garvin himself. Jon removed the man's gun holster from the bedpost, and Slocum set his .44 muzzle in his face.

"Wake up Garvin," Slocum ordered.

The man opened his eyes with a loud "Huh."

"Where is that damn Sears hiding at?"

"Hiding? How the hell should I know? Who are you fuckers?"

"You want to live to see that sun come up, you better remember."

"I swear I don't know. He quit me yesterday. Rode off. Said he was going to kill one sumbitch then go back to Texas. Hell, they all quit. Yellow-bellied sonsabitches."

"Was that your piebald horse?"

"Yeah, he owes me for him. Why?"

"He's dead, but Sears raped a woman and stole her horse now."

"He damn sure don't work for me no more. I don't have any help. They all run off."

"You better sell out and go yourself."

"Over my dead body is how I'll go."

"That ain't hard to arrange. A nickel's worth of lead would end your misery."

"Who the hell are you anyway? You blew up my horse pen, spooked off all my damn horses, put tin cans on their horse's tails, and caused more wrecks than an army could have set off."

"Folks are damn tired of your men running over them. They'll run off the next bunch you hire to do that, they know how now."

"Wait, leave me my gun. I'm defenseless without it."

"We'll hang it on the corral, but don't go get it before sun's up or we'll shoot you down out there."

"I won't."

"Garvin?"

"Yeah."

"You try running ranchers off again, wear your Sunday suit."

"Why?"

"So the funeral director don't have to bury you in rags," Slocum said.

The old man snorted out his nose with a loud grunt.

"You better heed my warning, old man. You won't last long running over folks again."

"We'll see about that."

"You hardheaded old bastard, listen to me. These folks will kill you the next time you try to ride over them."

Garvin acted like he never heard him. Carter reported that there was no one else around.

"What the hell is your real name?" Garvin asked.

"William Bonney," Slocum said.

"I heard about you. I knew you were some big-name outlaw. Well, Bonney, you can shoot me down now. If you don't, I'll be back here and nail your hide to my outhouse."

"Like a damn steer, Garvin, all you can do is try. Let's go, boys, he's through."

They started back, and Carter asked Jon to be excused since they had Garvin whipped.

"I want to go by and tell Helen the news. She's a real sweet lady and I'd like to help her some."

"You do that, Carter. Take a couple of days and you still have your job. I know Sis will appreciate you doing that too."

Carter saluted then and rode off in Helen's direction.

Slocum still wondered where Sears went. Had he gone back to Texas or was he lingering around looking for revenge? Good question to ask about a riled rattler. Only time would tell.

Their next trip to town, gossip told them that Garvin had caught a train out of there. Not a word to anyone about his business, but Slocum had it in the back of his mind the old man had gone for reinforcements. He told Glenna so.

"Don't count him out. He may be gathering help from down in that country he came from."

She hugged his arm as they headed for home with their supplies and the new dress finally done. "I hate that. You guys worked so hard to get them out. But I think he is like that and believes he can move us all out."

"I need to ride on soon, so you just be ready."

"I think Jon is going to lose Carter, don't you? He and Helen are getting close, aren't they?"

"She needs someone. I don't blame him. I don't reckon he's ever had a wife, and she would be good to him."

"I agree. So you're going to have to move on then."

He looked off at the distant horizon and then nodded. "Someone will put things together and say, 'Why, he's that Clark fellow out there at the Russell place.'"

"You know I am going to miss not having you to fuss with."

"I'll miss you, but one has to face reality. The longer I stay, the better their chances of finding me."

"What is that like? Never being able to trust anyone and always on the move?"

"It ain't fun and games, I can tell you that."

"You have money, don't you?"

"Enough to get by on."

She dropped her chin and shook her head. "I finally find someone tough enough to put up with me and I lose him."

He turned and kissed her cheek.

"That's what I mean. You are a real kisser and then you will go away like smoke." She threw her hands in the air like was she throwing out the dishwater. "Oh, brother, I will miss your easy ways loving me too, plus your company to go to church with me and take me to town. But yes, big man, in the end I will survive."

"Good."

Jon gave him the choice of horses and wouldn't take any money. He decided on Spook, and Jon agreed he would be the best for a long haul. He reshod him that week, putting off leaving. He planned to go out to Deadwood and then head west for the mountains for the summer. Maybe up in Wind River country—who knew.

Glenna realized he was going to leave soon, and she never bugged him about it. But while Jon was off checking cattle, she spent the morning sitting on a nail keg and visiting with him while he shod Spook. When he was halfway done with his job, she went and fetched a pail of water along with a dipper and watered the horse down.

"Hey, it's getting warm today, isn't it?" she said, handing him a dipper of water after he dried his sweaty face on a towel she had for him.

"Thanks," he said and winked at her. "You never had any suitors before your husband?"

"No, boys were boys to me. I never would have realized that Russell was interested in me, but he caught me away from the house and took my arm. He said, 'Let's you and I get married.'

"I looked at him like he was crazy. 'You want to marry me?' 'Hell yes,' he said. So I said, 'When?' 'Saturday night.' I thought what the hell, no one else wanted me. 'Sure,' I said, 'what do I have to do?'

" 'I guess just wear a Sunday dress.' he said. 'I've never been married.' That was it, we got married. Had a one-night honeymoon. I reckon he'd spent enough on floozies to know what to do with me. Monday morning I was fixing breakfast in the old soddy and my new husband rode off for three days to check on his cattle. I thought that was married life."

Slocum had the left front hoof in his lap, trimming on it. "Sounds exciting as hell."

"It was, but I didn't know any better. He hired Jon after

Dad died and we put our cattle with his. I got my back up and so they built me this house. Strange man, I am certain he frequented the cathouse in town when he was drinking. But, like I said, I had no measure of what a husband should do. Jon and I were together. We had the ranch, and we sold our old place to pay for my house. All I missed when Granger died was that feeling of contentment I got at the end of him being on me."

Slocum looked up and dropped the hoof. She tossed him the towel to dry his face again. Finished, he smiled. "That was some deal."

She tossed her hair back. "I could not believe that first night you and I had together that I had missed so damn much. Honest truth, I thought every wife had a husband like mine. Who didn't care or even think about his partner—just breed her and go to sleep. When I didn't get pregnant, I wondered what was wrong. I never found out what. He never cared, but he expected he'd get me with child if he tried harder, then later he gave up and I was simply his to rut with."

"You grew up a tomboy. No time for courting. You did miss a lot." He nailed the shoe on the front hoof then snipped the nails and finished that hoof.

"He will be fine tied there. Let's go have lunch, and you can finish him later."

"Sure," he said and put his arm on her shoulder.

"I'm going to miss that too. You being close to me."

He looked at the gathering clouds. "It's going to rain this evening."

"I bet so." She stopped at the front door and kissed him. "After lunch, before you go back to shoeing him, we need to honeymoon."

"I agree."

"You are so hard to convince." She snuggled to him as they crossed the yard.

It rained that afternoon, and at dawn, when he had Spook saddled and ready, everything dripped from the rainfall the night before. They had not slept much. But it had been a dreamy night, with bright flashes and rumbles of thunder to match their last flight together.

He kissed her, shook Jon's hand, and rode away, trying not to imagine her lithe, willowy body or the light perfume she wore—reminders that he'd left another terrific lady.

13

Deadwood was booming like he'd expected. But while he might have found some souls who knew him, United States marshals and Pinkerton pricks also hung out there, looking all the time for wanted men and fugitives who had escaped prisons. He wore a suit coat, white shirt, and string tie, plus a beard by then, so it might be less of a giveaway who he was. Card games there were crooked, but he could mark cards too, and in the confusion win some hands. John Clark was his name, and he found a room to share with a lady of the night named Sherry Taylor, whom he met in a hillside saloon on his second night in town. She was in her late twenties and had a soggy figure, but most men liked chubby women who weren't too fat. His roommate fit the bill, and she earned a few bucks more than common street women, enough to keep up her dope habit. She took cocaine more like it was aspirin, when in pain or when she was feeling despondent. Didn't matter which either.

He played cards till all hours, and by the time he got back to the room, she'd have sent her john for the night home or away somewhere. A few nights she sought his lovemaking instead of powder and said he was always rewarding to her. So their time went on until he knew he had to move on and took the stage to Cheyenne.

In Fort Laramie, he bought a horse, having sold Spook for a good profit up north in Deadwood. He had won a few hundred at gambling, so he was far from broke. He strapped his saddle on this new horse, a bay gelding about five, and set out. He hoped that his having bought a stage ticket to Cheyenne would throw them off track if they were on his heels—no telling—while in the meantime he rode north.

Spring was starting to bloom across the country. He met a Texas outfit who'd been wintering their cattle west of Fort Laramie, and the outfit's boss, Big Jim Caltron, a burly, gravel-voiced man in his forties, with a smile and large handshake.

"Where you headed?" Caltron asked after they had talked about several things in general.

"Not anywhere in particular. Why?"

"You look like a man who could deliver these cattle for me in Montana. I started out last summer, and when I got up here they warned me I might have snow all the way it was so late. So I bought a lot of hay from area farmers and brought these longhorns through the winter. But I need them driven up to Bozeman and sold. I've got a big ranch in Texas needs my attention and a wife I miss real bad. You said you'd taken cattle to Abilene and Wichita. Can't be any worse than that. You get them up there, sell them, pay the boys and take your share, then ship the rest to me by Wells Fargo—to my bank in San Antonio. I'll pay you four hundred bucks to handle the deal. Fair enough?"

Slocum sat under the flapping canvas shade and looked out across the new grass and wildflowers of the Wyoming countryside to the distant purple mountains. "I reckon you've hired yourself a trail boss."

They shook hands, and Caltron went for a bottle of good whiskey and two glasses. When he returned, Slocum held the glasses and Caltron poured it. "These boys are a little winter-weary, but they will work, and they know the business. I can show you my pay plan for them. I am damn sure glad I ran into you. You should get in on the early market. I don't know of too many herds this far north this early."

"Yes. We should be there well before any others. You know I'm not God, and we might have some tough storms to net us between here and there."

"Everything you do in this world has risk. Do the best you can and I'll understand. Send me some telegrams and let me know what is happening. Hell, I'll be two months getting home."

The whiskey was good. That evening after supper, he met the outfit's other leaders and then the rest of the men. They were all young and tough. Caltron had a rule that he'd fire you for fighting in camp or while on the job and wouldn't pay you a dime. That kept that from happening, as far as they were from home. Dan Black was his *segundo* and about twenty-two. Several of the boys were in their middle teens. Rack and Trumbo were Caltron's point men. They were athletes and horsemen, and Slocum could see them tending to directing the herd. An Indian boy was the horse wrangler, and they called him Chalk. Rufus Digby was the cook, an old army man who smoked a pipe and ran the camp. The rest of the boys Slocum still had to learn the names of.

"We were planning on leaving in two days. That suit you?" Caltron asked Slocum, sipping on a whiskey.

"Fine with me. I figure we are two months from where you want me to deliver them."

Caltron agreed. He left him a sheet of addresses and his bank's address too.

"I am going to catch a train east from Cheyenne, then take a riverboat and another train back west."

"Be careful so you make it."

"Oh, hell, I have to make it. I miss my lovely wife so damn much I can't even think about anything else."

"I know how you feel. We'll get them cattle up there and get them sold."

The next day, Caltron shook Slocum's hand and left. One of the boys took Big Jim to Fort Laramie to catch a stage and to bring his horse and saddle back to the camp.

The very next morning they were on the move. Rufus's two teams of mules, hitched to the chuckwagon and the half wagon on behind, had to be led the first mile, but they settled down. The steers, after the long winter, were placid and headed north for twelve miles that day. They lost one horse who had stepped into a badger hole and had to be destroyed. Slocum noted this in his new logbook. Jimmy Evans, the scout, found them a new camp for the next day and reported back in. He also told Slocum they had pine forest ahead and a mountain range that he'd learned about from a freighter. Slocum rolled out the map and they looked hard at it. The mountains were there, and he hoped they'd find graze, but they might have to drive farther than usual to find a suitable place to stop.

He thanked the boy, maybe almost eighteen years old. He had made a good hand for Caltron, and Slocum saw why. His trust in the hands grew as the days passed. On the drive to Billings, they were warned that the Crows would want a fee for crossing their land. As many as a dozen head of cattle. Slocum talked that over with Dan Black. They'd cut them out the limpers if they had to.

"But I'd rather not pay them a damn thing," Black said.

"Peaceful passage has a price," Slocum said. "Highway robbery is where I draw the line."

Black laughed. "This ain't your first cattle drive, is it?"

"Certainly not my first, and I hope not my last."

They both laughed then. One cowboy, Pete Combs, took sick on them. Rufus made him a bed in the trailer, and everyone thought he'd die. High fever and he was near out of his mind. But they were halfway across the Crow reservation when one day he got well enough to climb down and eat with them. A miracle, and his recovery cheered up the crew, especially when, in a few days, he was back on horseback.

Rufus treated two hands for boils on their butts and set one broken arm for a boy in a horse wreck. The old pipe-sucking ex-noncom was almost a surgeon in Slocum's book. His food wasn't as good as Murty's, but it was good enough to eat, and he cooked some really good elk meat on an occasion or two.

The Crows missed charging them a fee by not being in their camp, but Slocum and his men gave some poor, begging squaws a limper that could hardly walk. Everyone smiled. If Slocum hadn't feared they all had the clap, he'd have let the squaws entertain his boys.

They found enough graze north of Billings that Slocum split the crew and let half go to town the first night and the others the next, on his advance of three dollars each from Caltron's petty cash. They came home whooping and none were arrested. In the end they lost three days, but Slocum's help was acting much more alive on the job, and tales of beautiful whores and fantastic feats were the topic of the next week's drive.

"You sure know men, Slocum." Black shook his head. "I'd never have thought about shutting down for three days. But that one-night furlough did us more good than Christmas at home would have."

"Boys need to be boys sometimes."

"I agree. They've been new men all week. Caltron had you figured out pretty quick as the man for this job. I was dreading him piling this job on me. I knew I'd get scattered or the crew would quit. Man, they really missed home feeding hay all winter in the cold up here and all."

"I'd have allowed those squaws to screw our boys, down there on the Crow reservation, but I figured they all had the clap."

Black threw his head back and laughed. "What you worry the most about never happens, does it?"

"You're right."

The boys had got some letters from home at Billings too. One boy told them his letter said that someone else had got Caltron's wife pregnant while he was gone.

"What do you reckon he did about that?" Rufus asked Slocum, joining in the conversation.

"I'm glad I wasn't there for it," Slocum told him.

"Much as he loved her, you wouldn't think that would happen," Rack complained. "What do you think?"

"Any of you got a wife at home?" Slocum asked.

The heads of those gathered around the table shook.

"Ain't none of us married, Slocum."

"You ever leave a wife unattended long enough, there's a chance some sweet-talking guy is going to get in her britches. Trust me, temptation is always there."

They laughed.

"But he was so in love with her—"

"You heard me," Slocum said and shook his head.

"By damn, I get one, I won't leave her that long."

"Boys, we have about a heavy push ahead to get there. If you are going back to Texas, I want you to decide by then. Caltron told me if there wasn't six men to take the horses and wagon back, to sell everything. Otherwise I can issue you enough money for supplies to get it all back home."

"How long will it take us?" one boy asked.

"Three months. You will make better time than driving cattle, but I figure roughly that long."

"I'm going home," another said. "Somehow."

Slocum felt certain that enough would go home to be able to return Caltron's stock and gear to Texas. He wondered if Caltron had been more worried than he'd let on about his wife running around on him, which was why he was wanting to get back to her. Tough deal if she was pregnant. Slocum would probably never know how it turned out.

They were less than week from Bozeman when his scout Jimmy Evans came in early one afternoon. He could tell the young man was vexed when he dismounted up by the chuckwagon, where Slocum was looking over the books.

"What's wrong, Jim?"

"I think some hard cases are sizing us up. Maybe make a try to grab the herd."

"What did you see?"

"Last three days they've been using field glasses to watch us. I first didn't think nothing about it. But I had a look at them and they look like tough hombres, and I figure they may try to jump us and try to take the herd."

"Let me go get my field glasses. My horse is saddled, and we'll go see what we can learn about them. I sure appreciate you watching out for us. Things have been almost too quiet."

"I'd hate to holler fire and there only be smoke."

"No, that's your job, and I appreciate that your scouting has been all no-nonsense so far."

"Thanks. It's a great job and I have appreciated your trust in me."

"Rufus, tell Dan we're going to go check on a few things. Keep an eye out and a Greener handy."

"Aye, boss man. I'll put off my nap today."

"We may have trouble coming."

"I'll tell the boys too."

"Do that and be careful. We're so damn close I can smell it."

"Me too sir. You two be careful."

Glasses in his saddlebags, he followed Jim's lead. "They were on that hill over there when I saw them last. Should we circle around back?"

"Good idea. Don't push too fast; we might run into them." Slocum motioned for Jim to lead the way.

In a short while, they found tracks coming and going. Both men nodded, and Jim led the way though the jack pines until they heard running water and could smell campfire smoke. They dismounted, hitched their horses and proceeded on foot. From a high point, they bellied down, and both men used their field glasses.

The camp was made up of some old brown sidewall tents, around which several squaws worked fixing food. The men were mostly half-breeds, except for one black-bearded, heavy-set white man who looked like he ran things.

"I wonder who he is," Jimmy said.

"I sure have no idea, but he looks like he doesn't earn a living doing anything."

Jimmy agreed. "But can we do anything before they try to take the herd?"

"Be sort of hard. I wonder if the law would come up and check on them for us."

"We could ask them to."

"Why don't you ride over and ask the law and explain what they've been doing?"

"I can do that. Might get us some help, huh?"

Slocum figured that with his beard and with everyone calling him Clark, his disguise as John Clark should hold with the law. The bunch he was watching could run off some of his cattle, but he doubted they could take the whole herd. Still, there was no need in taking any chances. He gave Jim some money for expenses. In the old days he'd have shot the camp up, run off their horses, and ended that matter. But things were getting a lot tighter in the West. Vigilante law was getting frowned on more and more.

With Jim gone to ask for help, Slocum rode back to camp. He'd have Dan scout ahead the next day, and he'd also keep an eye out for any sign of the breeds preparing to raid the herd. When they came in for supper, he told the men about the problems they might face and to be watchful. While the herd was trail-broke, they'd be hell to ever reassemble if they were stampeded in this timber country.

Everyone agreed, and being so close to their destination, they were pissed that anyone would try to block them from getting there. It had been way over a year since they'd left home.

Buyers had begun to show up. When Slocum got back from scouting for trouble, two men were there talking about buying half the herd and giving a paper for the rest until they got the first half sold.

Slocum told the pair he'd sell them the whole herd or part of it, but he could take no paper for the cattle. He had to sell them for cash for his boss in Texas.

"What would you take for them?" the one partner, Simpson, asked.

"What's the going market?"

"Oh, ten cents on the hoof."

"Hell, I got more than that back in Abilene years ago."

"I imagine you could get twenty cents."

"If that's the market. How many do you want?"

"We'd need to buy them cheaper than that to make any money."

"You said that was the market," he reminded the man.

His partner jumped up. "I can see we can't do any business here."

"Sorry we came out," Simpson said.

Dan Black, who'd been on guard duty all day, had come in and heard their offer. "They didn't want to buy cattle, did they?"

"Only to steal them. What did you learn?"

"They watched us through their glasses a lot is all I can say."

At dark Jim arrived back with three deputies. They ate with the crew.

"You seen any more activity from the breeds?" the lead man, Ables, asked.

"They're still scoping us all day," Black told him.

"We've got warrants for some of them, and Jim said he could take us to their camp. They ain't struck you by morning, we'll go arrest a passel of them," the deputy said.

Slocum thanked them for coming, and they were up at daybreak, with no raid. So Slocum and Jim rode back to the breeds' camp with them. A few shots fired in the air, and the breeds surrendered without a fight.

Slocum asked the big white guy in irons why he'd been scoping the herd.

"Aw we were only looking. Too goddamn many cows to steal."

Slocum thanked the deputies, and he and Jim rode back to catch up with the herd.

Close to town they settled the herd for a stay, and Slocum went into Bozeman to find a buyer or two. It was a typical mining town, wide open 24/7, and things buzzing. Everyone trying to get a winning business going on the upswing. Everything from a millinery to dress shops, saloons galore, and plenty of whorehouses to keep the miners right there and broke. And a few blocks of nothing but narrow crib houses with scantily dressed women standing at their doors calling out for business in bawdy terms: "Hey, you with the long dick. Come fuck me."

Past them, Slocum stabled his horse, took a room in the Montana Queen Hotel, and walked a block down to the Great North Saloon. A palace-like place with gaslights and sharp hostesses in low-cut dresses who met you at the door and offered you their services in an upstairs bed with clean sheets. "The cost is nominal during the daylight hours, sir."

"I am really here on business. Any cattle buyers in here?"

"Some of the best are playing poker right over there." She began to escort him over to a table of players.

"And you are drinking what?"

"A cold beer."

"And your name is?"

"Clark, John Clark."

"Your beer is coming. Gentlemen, this is John Clark," she said to the players. "He is looking for cattle buyers."

"Have a seat, Clark. You might change my luck," said the big man smoking a cigar and dealing cards. "You're in the next hand. How many head you got?"

"Twenty-five hundred head."

The big man frowned. "Where in the hell have they been?"

"My boss wintered them in Wyoming."

"Who's he?"

"Jim Caltron, he had to go back to Texas, and I'm in charge."

The cigar man took the stogie out of his mouth, laid it in an ashtray, and put down the deck. "They have any meat on them?"

"Yes, we've come easy and they're fleshy."

"I'll be there in the morning. Where you at?"

"Oh, east of here in some grass."

"I'll meet you at six o'clock at the restaurant, Cook's Place, and I'll feed you before we go look."

"What are cattle worth up here?"

"What do you say to fifteen cents a pound?"

"That sounds good, but I think we can get more."

The man drew his breath out of his nose. "Eighteen."

Men around the table were so intent on the big man's words that it became very quiet under the hissing lamp overhead.

"You need twenty-five hundred head?" Slocum asked him

"I can damn sure handle them if they ain't skeletons."

"I ain't got any reason to lie to you. You can see for yourself. My boss fed these cattle good last winter down there. We been coming ten miles a day to hold that flesh on them, and the graze we been on has been strong. They've been licking hair on their sides ever since I took over."

"You been up here before?"

"No, sir. But I think it was time for me to get here."

"There ain't hardly any head of beef around here to buy worth slaughtering. I can sure use them. I have a railroad construction beef contract and two mines to feed."

"I reckon tomorrow we can talk business."

"I reckon we can." He picked up his hand and after a quick look tossed it in. "Who needs cards?"

"I never caught your name."

"Alexander, Cy Alexander."

"Nice to meet you. I'll raise a dollar and take two." Poor old Caltron might have wife troubles in Texas, but in a few days he'd damn sure not have any money problems. That would be over three hundred thousand dollars. That wasn't even real. And Slocum had three of a kind in his hand—sevens. He won the pot and everyone moaned.

"Damn. He walks in, sells his damn cattle, and cleans us out. Texas welcome to Montana, Clark."

"Thanks, gents, I can use some good news."

"How long you been trailing them?" another player asked.

"Long enough. He hired me at Fort Laramie to bring them up here."

Alexander nodded. "Next herd coming is in Colorado. I got a wire today. How did you get by all the lookouts?"

"I have no idea. We just headed up here. I had my boss's maps. We never had any trouble, except some breeds scouted us until the sheriff arrested them."

"No stampedes?"

"No, sir, we just came up along the trail. Those cattle were drove far last year. Caltron wintered them on real good hay so they'd be in shape, and he waited till the grass was strong enough to head them up here."

"He got a big ranch in Texas?"

"You know I don't know. I have never been to his place down there. Like I said we met in Fort Laramie country, and he hired me to ramrod this deal on up here."

"He must have trusted you."

"We hit it off. I'd driven cattle to Abilene out of Texas, and Caltron had some good hardworking boys." He held a pair of aces in his hand. So he raised the bet a dollar and discarded two to disguise his aces.

"Mister, if I had a herd of cattle, I think I'd trust you to get them here, but that many—whew."

"Good help. No outlaws. It all went good."

"What'll he do with all that money?" another asked.

Slocum shook his head. "I ain't sure. I guess just enjoy it."

They all laughed. He wound up his card playing at eleven and headed for his hotel room. The lady who'd introduced him to the buyer, and to whom he owed a tip, must have had a customer to service, since he didn't see her when he left. The night was cool, and he wondered if someone had been spying on him as he crossed the street. It was no time to have problems. Maybe by the next day he'd have some good words to send to Caltron by telegram.

He was walking toward his hotel in the night's shadows when a bullet shattered the glass window of the store right beside him. He dove behind a horse trough for cover. Two more shots followed. Gun in hand, he rose up to look in the direction the shots had come from—across the street from him. A shotgun-bearing marshal came running down the boardwalk, shouting, "Hold your fire. Hold your fire."

Satisfied that the shooter was gone, Slocum got to his feet.

"Who did it?"

"Shots came from over there." Slocum pointed to the place beside a dark shop across the street.

"You didn't see him?"

"I didn't see anything but the flash of a shot and took cover behind the trough."

"You have any enemies?"

"I don't know. I have only been here for about six hours."

"Make anyone mad or get in a fight tonight?"

"I am a drover. I came to town to sell my cattle and I found a man to buy them. Played some cards. I have no idea why I was shot at."

"Mr. . . . ?"

"John Clark, Sweetwater, Texas."

"I need to write that down now."

"Sure. I feel bad about this broken glass, but I can't figure who was wasting bullets on me."

"Mr. Clark, we consider our town a safe place to live. Shooting makes everyone nervous, you understand. I will need lots of information so we can prevent this happening again."

"I understand, but I have a business meeting at six A.M. to sell my cattle, so make it as brief as you can."

"I understand. My partner is the guy running up here now so don't concern yourself about that."

"Thank you. Being shot at is unnerving."

"I agree. This is Marshal Hart. Sir, this is John Clark. He was shot at. He has only been here six hours and was shot at."

"Anyone contacted Ira Counts about his broken window?" Hart asked.

"No. If you can do that, I'll stay here till he gets someone to watch things."

"You have enough from me?" Slocum asked.

"If I need more—"

"I will be either here at the Montana Queen Hotel or with the large herd out east of here."

"Thank you."

At the hotel, Slocum asked the desk clerk to wake him at six. A chair against the doorknob, he woke up when the clerk knocked. He called a thank-you. Dressed, he met Alexander in the café, and they ate a breakfast of eggs, ham, hash browns with biscuits and gravy, plus coffee.

"They say someone shot at you last night?" Alexander asked.

"Crazy deal. I was walking back to the hotel and a shot rang out. I dropped off to hide behind a horse trough, and the shooter sent two more at me. I never saw him or heard what he wanted. He shot out a large window in a store."

"Might be settling an old score?"

"Have no idea." Slocum shrugged his shoulder. It could have been mistaken identity—the shooter thinking he was someone else—but he believed it more likely that he knew the shooter or the shooter knew him. He would have to be more careful.

At the livery, he got his horse and Alexander got his. Two men who worked for Alexander joined them—a tall man named Ulmer and another, older man called Olsen. They trotted out to where the men held the herd.

Rufus made them fresh coffee. Slocum could tell that as he rode into camp Alexander was impressed by the cattle's condition. After the coffee break he and his two men rode through the grazing herd looking to be sure there weren't many questionable beeves blended in. Alexander rode back to the camp and dismounted.

"They are great cattle. He hired the right man to drive them up here. We can weigh about six to seven hundred head a day and put them on some rangeland I own. That means driving in about that many to the scales each day. So in about three to four days they will all be weighed. I will settle with you the following day at the Silver National Bank. That's going to be lots and lots of money."

"I know, and Wells Fargo can get it to Texas for my boss and put it in his San Antonio bank. I am not worrying about that. These boys have been gone from home almost two years, and they have earned their wages. They are some of the best men I have ever worked with. They have never complained since I joined them and took over for Jim Caltron."

Alexander shook his head. "That is amazing, but I say your boss, you, and these men have done a wonderful job. I did not believe these cattle could be in the shape they are. When those other cattle get here later, they won't be in near the same shape as these are."

"Where do we deliver tomorrow?"

"The scales are at the railroad depot. They have certified scales and are bonded."

"Good. We can find it. I'll send my scout in to find it today and make the way."

"I know you can handle it." Alexander shook his head. "If you ever need work, look me up."

"Thank you."

After Alexander and his men left, Slocum explained their needs to Dan, the two point men, and his scout, Jimmy Evans, so they could figure out the route. They would be delivering six hundred head in the morning.

The men smiled and reassured Slocum that they'd find everything and do it right.

He also wrote out a telegram to Caltron in Texas. He was about to sell his cattle for a large sum, and if all went well, in five days Slocum would send the money via Wells Fargo to Caltron's bank in San Antonio. He turned to Rufus as Jimmy and the two point men rode off to set the route. The old man had reloaded and lit his pipe and was shaking out the match.

"I figured we'd get up here and sell the cattle," Rufus said. "It's been a long time getting here, but Caltron culled all the bad apples out of this crew before we got to Colorado. He treated us all well. I sure hated him to have any trouble at home about his wife, but those may have been rumors. I am not that good with math. What will these group bring?"

"Three hundred thousand dollars plus."

The older man had a belly laugh going. Caught coughing and choking next, he had to take the crooked stem pipe out of his mouth. Still laughing, he shook his head. "That much money he can buy a new one."

Slocum was laughing too. "Yes, he can."

"His plan worked, but he never could find anyone tough enough to run it until he found you."

Slocum looked around. "You know I'm going to pay you and Dan twelve hundred dollars each, which includes you and him taking the boys and Caltron's wagon, mules, and horses home. I am setting aside that much for food too, and you can give Caltron back what you don't use. The boys will get six hundred dollars each for their two years' work and no deductions for any treats or advances he or I gave them."

"Sure fair enough. I guess most are going home with me."

"Two boys are all that are going to be looking around and not going back."

"They'll have enough money to do what they want."

Slocum nodded.

"Someone heard you were shot at last night. You know who did it?"

"A damn poor shot, thank God."

"You get lots more funny now this job is close to over."

"I have no idea who wants me dead. Glad he didn't get it done. What will you do back in Texas?"

"That money will buy me a small place. I'll have some relatives live on it, and when I get too old to do this kind work, I'll have a shelter."

"Good idea."

"I've been planning on it that way."

Slocum looked off at the towering mountains and wondered where he'd spend his old age. No telling, but if he kept getting shot at, he might not have to worry about it. The shooter idea bothered him more than he wanted to let on. Knowing who he was up against was number one on his list.

Maybe the town law had found out something—but he doubted it. He nodded when Rufus offered him more coffee.

Pete rode in and left his horse at the rope hitch line.

"We heard you sold the steers."

"We shook hands. Delivery starts in the morning. It will take a few days to weigh them all. But inside of a week Rufus will be trailing you all south for Texas."

"Boy, I ever get back to Texas, I'll never leave again."

"You aren't far from starting back."

"They say someone shot at you?"

"I guess everyone's heard it now. I don't know who it was, but thank God he missed."

"He messes with you, he may get messed with by all of us."

Slocum held up his hand. "I don't want anyone hurt."

"We can handle ourselves, boss man."

"Thanks. But don't get too involved. I'll be on my guard."

"We're going to back you. I mean it."

"Maybe we can all get out of here in a few days and nothing will come of it. Thanks, Pete."

When Pete left, Rufus spoke softly behind him. "That shooting at you pissed all the crew off. I mean they heard about it and they were mad as hell."

"I appreciate them, but it no doubt is my problem."

"They ain't going to let anything happen to you, trust me."

Slocum decided to go back into town. He was not looking for any trouble, but a night or two in a real bed, maybe some cards and the lady he owed for her introduction to

Alexander all were on his mind. And maybe the shooter might show up.

"Tell Jim Evans and Dan to pick a crew, and them plus the point riders take the first six hundred head into town and to the scales if I am not back in the morning."

Rufus saluted him. "Can do, sir."

Slocum rose to go back to town. He was surprised that he never met the boys who were after him on the road. His horse in the stables, he went and found supper in a café. The food was rich beef stew and sourdough biscuits with home-made butter and chokecherry jam. He tipped the waitress, paid the bill, and went across the street to the saloon. He had noted that the store window behind him was boarded up, no doubt waiting for replacement glass.

Alexander wasn't there at the card table, and the hostess Slocum had met was not in sight. He spoke to another woman working the floor.

"There was a lady here last night with light brown hair that did me a favor?"

"They ever find who shot at you?"

"No, ma'am."

"You must mean Audrey. I think she is occupied right now. But I will get her word that you wish to speak to her."

"I'd appreciate that."

"Does she know your name?" she asked.

"The drover named Clark."

"I will do that, Mr. Clark. Can I do anything else for you?"

"No, I'll play cards here for a while."

"Fine. Good to meet you, Mr. Clark. My name is Belle if you need me."

"Well, the cattle salesman is here," one of the players said teasingly.

"When does the sale start?" another asked.

Slocum nodded. "We start in the morning." He took a seat and put some money on the table. His hat set back, he settled in the chair facing the front door and waited for the dealer to deal the next hand.

"They find the guy shot at you?"

Slocum shook his head.

"Strange deal, you get here and some one shoots at you."

Slocum agreed and the conversation died out.

He won and lost some small pots. Keeping about even, he continued to play and drew a better hand. Three queens, and he tried for four, drawing two cards. It gave him a pair of fives and a full house that should win. He stayed with the betting and in the end won a nice pot.

Audrey came by and quietly spoke to him. He excused himself and stepped back to talk to her. His voice low, he said, "I owe you for last night. I sold the herd I drove up here to Mr. Alexander this morning."

"Oh, you did well."

"I have fifty dollars for you for putting me in touch with him."

"Can we celebrate later?"

"Sure."

"I will be here when you finish, if that is all right?"

"Fine. I'll play a few more hands."

"I have a fine room upstairs to use."

"I appreciate your offer."

"No problem." She smiled mischievously, and he kissed her cheek.

"You in this hand, Lucky?" a player asked.

"You bet."

"Then ante up five dollars so we can start."

Settled in the chair, he tossed in his ante and settled down.

"You want a drink?" Audrey whispered.

He shook his head. In case the shooter came back, he would need all his senses about him to defend himself. "Thanks."

The hostess setup in this place impressed him. Not many saloons or whorehouses had this hostess system. None of the women that worked the floor here were dumb or crazy-acting. They were polite, intelligent, and not brassy, and he wondered if he'd stepped into a new world in Montana.

Cards came and went. About ten, he excused himself and took Audrey's arm when she came by. They ascended the carpeted stairs and soon were in a room with red velvet drapes and low lights. Once they were behind the shut door, he kissed her on the mouth and she filled his arms.

"Tell me the going price."

"Oh, we get a hundred dollars for full evening."

"I can afford that."

"I should have told you that before we came up here."

"No, I knew the service was high-priced. I just appreciated you introducing me to Alexander."

"He sent me a thank-you note and money too. So two people are happy."

"He frequent you or your others?"

"No. He must have a fine wife. He has never been upstairs."

"I don't have a wife, fine or otherwise."

"Are you going to unhook my dress?"

"Certainly."

"Do you always drive cattle to markets?"

"When I can get the work."

His unhooking released the silky gown and exposed her pear-shaped breasts. She stepped out of the dress and went to hang it up on a hanger in the closet.

"How did you get here?" he asked.

"My husband was killed in a mine accident. I faced a rather poor life as a widow. It was not an easy choice, but I was promised good pay and protection from anyone who might be a threat to me. This is not a slave situation, nor is anyone punished for refusing a customer. I would not be here otherwise."

"Would you leave if someone gave you a legitimate door to escape?" He was holding her loose in his arms.

"I would be very cautious until I knew it was real."

He shook his head and kissed her softly. "I have no passageway from here to offer, but I am pleased to get to share you tonight. I only was curious."

"You have a story too. You are educated and are out of place as a drover."

He nodded and pressed her body to him. "But I am one, and do it as seriously as you do your job."

She nodded, and they were soon lost in their quest for a sexual union on top of the bed. Her subtle body, smooth skin, and willingness all swept him away.

14

Before dawn, he ate breakfast in the nearby café and then checked his horse out of the livery. He was on the road as daylight crept over the horizon of mountains. When he reached the herd area, he could hear the cattle protesting as they were gathered for the first drive. Things were going well; his scout and Dan were in charge, and the bell steer was out in front waiting with patience to lead the others to the scales. Several cowboys were holding the rest of the herd back so they didn't try to go with the ones they'd cut out to be weighed.

Slocum sat his horse and watched the operation go forward smoothly. Then he rode on to the chuckwagon and dismounted to speak to Rufus.

"They have it in hand," he said to his cook.

"Good boys." He relit his pipe. "Yesterday they got a lead on the shooter."

"Oh?" Slocum nested the cup of coffee in his hand.

"They think his name is Sears. That ring a bell?"

"I had some problems with him in Nebraska. He up here?"

"Pete and Benny are looking for him around town right now."

"Should I go back and help them?"

Rufus shook his head. "The boys say they can handle him. He won't shoot at you again."

"I told them—"

"These boys are damn grateful for you getting them up here and selling the cattle. They made up their minds to handle this at the first word of that attack."

"I don't want—"

"Just leave it to them. Cattle are going to the pens."

"I . . . Oh, okay. And yes, the cattle operation looks good. Thanks."

Three hours later, when he rode into town, they were weighing five head of cattle at a time. Things were going smoothly. He and Alexander meet in the office and discussed the operation.

"You have some great men," Alexander said.

"Good hands."

"What will you do after the sale is completed?"

"Oh, I guess wander back south."

"Texas?"

"I have no big place to land."

"I could offer you a job as a buyer."

Slocum looked out the dirty window as another five steers were driven by going to the pasture. "Thanks, but it will be fall soon and I aim to get somewhere warmer."

"You ever need work, I can find you a job."

"I appreciate that."

"No problem. You realize the next major herd won't be here until fall?"

"I considered it."

"What about the man owns these ones?"

"I knew him only a few days. Nice guy, with problems at home I guess."

"You heard from him?"

"I will today. I sent him the sale information by telegram yesterday."

Alexander nodded. He and Alexander shook hands, and Slocum excused himself. He saw Pete and another cowboy ride by. He wondered if they'd found Sears. He'd know before the day was over what had happened.

The cattle all penned and being weighed by a certified agent of the railroad, Slocum went and caught one of the men and told him of his plan to round up the rest of men to go eat lunch before they rode back to camp.

Then he went to the telegraph office on the other end of the depot.

"Any message for Clark?"

"Yes, we have one, sir."

Dear Clark

You are super. I never expected that much per pound but I can, like every one, use the money. I agree on the payment to you and the men. Tell them I have work in Texas. I will watch for your telegram when you settle.

God bless you.
Jim Caltron

Slocum nodded and thanked the man in the visor.

Outside he gathered his horse, and the crew all went to their mounts. On their way to lunch, Pete turned to Slocum and nodded. "That back-shooter won't bother anyone again."

"Thanks." He didn't know or care about the how or the when. The matter was settled.

They had a nice lunch in the main café and rode back together, the boys acting like schoolboys let out for vacation.

"We're three days from settling. It will be fun," he said to Dan.

"Rufus said you weren't going back with us?"

"I have some things to do."

"I figured we'd have a big party going home."

"No reason not to."

"Jim was good, Boss, but you—well we really enjoyed your job of heading us up here."

"It went well."

"Rufus said you took good care of us too."

"You boys will be paid well. No deducts. You get foreman wages too."

"That's great."

"Jim Caltron is pleased too."

"Man, it will be good to see Texas."

Slocum nodded.

The next two days the rest of the cattle were weighed and the matter settled. Two thousand, four hundred and twenty steers. They averaged a weight 860 pounds each and a value of $154.80 apiece. Over three hundred sixty five thousand in total. He would pay the cowboys six hundred dollars apiece. Rufus, Dan, and Slocum were going to receive twelve hundred apiece and that same amount was to be held to pay for the cost of going-home supplies.

He brought both Dan and Rufus to the bank for the settlement, and money was put into an envelope for each of the men. The Wells Fargo man assured Slocum that the remaining money would be transferred to Jim Caltron's account in San Antonio. He also gave him a receipt for what the bank was mailing to Caltron.

Slocum shook everyone's hand, thanked Alexander, then the three rode back to camp. The boys said they didn't need to stay there any longer, and they started to load up so that

they could head for Wyoming first thing the next morning.
Two of the punchers left them and went their own way.

On the trail the next morning. there followed good days
tending to the and wrangling the horses. As they neared
Fort Laramie, Slocum shook everyone's hand and left them
for his lone ride to Glenna's place. When he rode up, she
came out of the house blinking her eyes and using the side
of her hand to shade the glare. "Is that you?"

"It ain't his brother, darling."

"Oh my, I never thought I'd see you alive again." She was
in his arms crying and hugging him. They were soon kissing and trying to smother each other.

"Where have you been?"

"Montana. Took a herd up there and sold them. Highest-
priced cattle I ever sold in my life."

"How much did you get for them?"

He whirled her around. "Eighteen cents a pound."

She whistled through her front teeth. "Gee that is high.
Put me down. I'll make us some coffee."

He looked around. "You expecting anyone?"

"No. Oh yes, we can drink coffee later, can't we?"

He hugged her again. "Much later."

15

They were at the table eating supper, Jon, Glenna, and Slocum, enjoying her meal. Carter wasn't there.

"She told you Carter and Helen are getting married?" Jon said and passed him the green beans.

"Yes and good."

"They are very happy," Glenna said.

"He is delighted, and now I'm looking for a new ranch hand." Jon shrugged. "He'll be hard to replace. You ever cut Sears's trail again?"

"I think he shot out a store window in Montana trying to kill me."

"Glad he missed," Glenna said and put her hand on top of his.

"So was I, but I had no idea it was him. Those cowboys who worked for me found him, and when it was over, all they said was—he won't bother me ever again."

"Did they kill him?" she asked.

"I suppose so. They were furious, and I was busy selling cattle, so they handled it. Has Garvin come back yet?"

"Not that we know about. But I'd expect him anytime if he went to Texas like he said he was going to do."

"It will pay to keep an ear out for him. He'll want revenge, and he's the kind that will exact it."

"You going to hang around?" Jon asked.

"Not for long. I can stay a couple of weeks."

Glenna smiled, pleased. "Good. There, Jon, you have some help."

"Maybe I can hire someone by then. Cowboys are hard to find. Carter could rope either end of a critter. Some of these guys who come looking for work can't even use a lariat."

Slocum nodded.

The next day he set out with Jon to check cattle. They found a longhorn cow in a bog. Jon went to shaking his head at the sight of the muddy cow who had wallowed around until she was totally mud-coated and mad, belly-deep in the bog. He dismounted and began to undress. "You get the job on land. I'll push on her."

"Fine, but remember when she comes out, she'll be madder than a hornet and blame us." Slocum laughed, shaking loose his lariat. They were in for lots of trouble with an angry cow and plenty of mud.

Jon waded in when Slocum had her caught by the horns. His ranch horse was ready to drag her out, but there was more than that to do. With her belly-deep in the mud, it was holding her too. The first pull, with Jon twisting her tail and getting more sloppy mud on himself, didn't budge her. Slocum got Jon's horse and tossed another rope on the noisy, bawling, protesting cow. He then led the horse along with his own and they both strained, pulling hard.

"Go! She's coming!" Jon shouted. The rope pressed hard on Slocum's right leg as both horses strained until the cow came loose and the horses pulled her sliding on her side through the mud. When she was clear, Slocum undid the rope from Jon's saddle and let go of his dally. The cow was on her feet and ready to charge them.

She slipped and fell down on her side, which gave Slocum a head start. He and his mount were off in a hard lope, and mama cow, hoarsely bawling, was up and after him like a Mexican fighting bull. He put spurs to the horse and felt like he was really leaving the country if she didn't let up. And it looked to Slocum like she'd wear both ropes till she wore them out.

Finally she gave up and ran off, and Slocum went back to get Jon.

When he found him, Jon had already caught his horse and, in his mud-caked underwear, was mounting up.

"Get my clothes and gun, I'm going home for a bath."

"And some new ropes." Slocum laughed at the sight of him. "You look like a chocolate candy." He gathered Jon's things, and they rode back.

At the ranch it was all Glenna could do not to laugh about her brother's condition. "Were you making mud pies?"

While Jon was bathing, a rider came by the place.

"Joel Wynn, this is John Clark," Glenna said to introduce them. "What brings you over here, Joel?"

"Nice to meet you. I just got word. Garvin is back with six hard cases from Texas."

"That's bad news," Slocum said. "Worse than a cow in a bog. How did you hear about it?"

"Rediford Moore was in town when they arrived on the train yesterday. Said the old man rented a wagon to haul them out to his place yesterday afternoon, and they were all hard cases."

"Any names for them?"

"No, he just saw them arrive then go by wagon to Garvin's ranch."

"We sure thank you for coming by," Glenna said. "Keep us informed. It don't sound good."

Wynn agreed. "Tell Jon for me. I'll get on."

"Thanks."

"You timed it right," she said. "Here we go again."

Slocum closed his eyes. *That old sumbitch didn't listen.*

Meetings were called for folks to gather at the schoolhouse, and protection groups were formed. One man had spoken to the sheriff, who said his hands were tied until they broke the law. Everyone waited for something to happen. Slocum made a few trips west and scoped out the operation at Garvin's. The men were trying to round up his ranch horses and not having lots of success. But in time they'd have something to ride, he decided, slipping back from his lookout point and going to his horse.

Saturday night, he and Jon checked out the saloons in town. They found a few gunmen here and there, drinking beer, which meant, Slocum figured, they didn't have money for whiskey. They were tight-lipped and stayed together in the places they landed.

Slocum picked out two of the younger ones, and when they started to leave, he stopped them.

"You boys work for Garvin?"

"Yeah, what business is it to you?"

"That old man tell you about his last men?"

"No, what happened to them?" the cocky one asked.

"Most of them caught freights out of here to save their asses. Folks up here don't take to strong-arm tactics. When you start, there will be repercussions."

"What the hell is that?" he asked his buddy.

"Means they will get back at us," his buddy said.

"Yeah, we'll have our own," the first one told Slocum.

Slocum looked off into the night and the dark street. "Take my word, you've been warned."

"Who the hell are you?"

"A man who hates to see folks killed."

In the saddle the kid jerked his horse around.

"Hey," Slocum said, "ask the old man where his last hands went."

"Fuck you, mister."

Slocum shook his head. "You've been warned."

The two young men rode off grumbling to each other.

"You warned them," Jon said, joining him.

"I just want to cut them off before they start hurting anyone."

"Maybe they came to be cowboys."

Slocum shook his head. "Garvin expects revenge."

"They won't be easy to run off."

Slocum stepped in the saddle and turned his horse. "We will see what we can do about encouraging them to leave."

"When will they make a move?"

"That is what I wonder." Slocum booted his horse into a trot, and they headed back to the ranch.

It was in Slocum's mind that they'd first start strong-arming the weakest—old folks, widows, and anyone who would be afraid. Garvin knew them and he'd start there.

All he and Jon could do was be aware and shut it down when it started.

They rode over to Carter and Helen's place. The two newlyweds looked very happy, and Helen hugged both of their visitors.

"What brings you two over here?" Carter asked, inviting them in for coffee.

"Slocum thinks that Garvin will start on the weakest and not realize you two are married. He has ten or twelve new hands. We spoke to two Saturday night in town. They are pretty cocksure. We don't want either of you hurt."

"Is Sears with them?" Helen asked.

Slocum shook his head. "To the best of my knowledge, Sears isn't on this earth anymore. He apparently tried to ambush me up in Montana, and the cowboys working for me got so mad they sent him to the happy hunting grounds."

"Good riddance," Carter said and hugged his wife.

"Just be careful," Jon said. "We don't know what they will do first, but he didn't hire them to simply ride herd."

"What are they doing now?"

"Looking all over hell for that remuda of his that we cut loose four months ago."

Slocum shook his head. "Those two rode some old horses into town last Saturday night. Their muzzles were snow-white."

They all laughed. "Why, those horses are scattered from here to hell by now," Carter said.

"Just be careful. We'll come on a moment's notice."

After coffee they hugged Helen and shook Carter's hand. Then they started home. No cows were bogged down that day in the wetlands.

"There ain't any way you could stay around here for a long while is there?" Jon asked as they rode.

"How is that?"

"You and my sister get along good. I ain't making light about that. But you and I fit like a glove and think a lot alike. We don't make lots of money running cows, but we do make some. You act kind a relaxed while you're here. I was thinking you might stay . . ."

"Love to, except some bounty hunter would figure out my disguise and come a-hunting me."

"Damn shame. I really enjoy having you."

They reined up when they saw a fire in the distance. Looked like a branding fire. They rode up on the ridge and got out their field glasses. Three men had a calf tied down bawling and were putting the iron to him.

"That damn sure ain't their calf," Jon said. "That roan cow is one of ours. I'd know her anywhere."

They put the glasses away, jerked rifles out of their

scabbards, and set their horses downhill to stop the thieves. Half the distance away from them, the rustlers began to shoot at them with their pistols, but the range was too far for pistols. Slocum and Jon spurred their horses as the rustlers tried to get mounted on their gun-spooked horses.

One rider was thrown over his horse's head, hard onto the ground. With a rifle shot Slocum wounded another as he tried to get away. The third one lost his struggle with his horse and the pony ran off before he could even get on it.

Slocum had no doubt these were Garvin's men. He had Jon take care of the two at hand and rode out to get the wounded man still on his horse, who had stopped. He was bent over in the saddle, not moving.

As he approached him, Slocum shoved the rifle in under his leg and drew his pistol. Cocked and ready, he rode in close and jerked the man's gun out of his holster. When he did, the man finally made an attempt to swing at him. Slocum turned his horse around and in a swift move busted the outlaw on the head, caved in his hat, and sent him facedown onto the ground.

"You should never have tried that, stupid." Then he recognized him as one of the ones he had spoken to on the saloon porch. "I told you not to stay."

16

Long past dark Jon and Slocum rode into the ranch and dropped heavy from the saddle. Glenna brought a candle lamp. "Where in the hell have you two been?"

"It's a long story," Slocum said, undoing his latigos.

"But we got a damn good alibi." Jon hoisted his saddle and pads off his horse.

"What's the alibi?"

"We caught three of Garvin's men putting his brand on ole Roan's calf in broad daylight."

"You what?" She frowned at Slocum.

"Let's see . . . one has a broken arm. He got thrown off his horse. One I shot trying to get away and he also has a bad headache from trying to fight me. Third one I guess got off unscathed, but they are all in the county jail. Sheriff is riding out and threatening Garvin with arrest 'cause he considers him a party to the rustling. It will send the rest packing."

"Helen and Carter said to tell you hello," Jon added.

"They happy?"

"They act that way, don't they, Slocum?"

"Happy as two peas in a pod." They laughed.

"Well, tell me, how did you find the rustlers?"

"We saw a fire far off and rode over the hill."

Glenna shook her head as they headed for the house. "You think it is over? Are we safe now?"

"Do I think that old man will give up? No. But he won't get any help out of his new hired thugs after today. The sheriff is upset enough to threaten him over the rustling because it was with his brand they were using."

"I have food still warm. I was expecting you long ago."

"We'll wash up and be there." They put their horses in the corral to roll in the dust, even as tired as they were. It had been a long day. Slocum's lower back told him so as well.

After the meal, Jon told them good night and went off to the bunkhouse. When he was gone, she came over and sat in his lap.

"You must be dead tired."

He kissed her. "I am."

"The sheriff still thinks you're Clark?"

"I think so. He was impressed that we apprehended those boys. He knew they were gunhands, not ranch hands."

"Can you stay for a while?"

"I think so."

"Good. Let's go to bed. You need some rest. I can curl around you and hold you tonight."

"Good deal."

"You know I'll miss you again when you leave. Like I did last time you rode off."

"You won't be alone. Let's try to sleep."

The next day word was out. Ranchers were coming by wondering what it would take to get rid of Garvin.

They were his employees and using his brand—that was the case they all presented.

"We all need to ride over there with a lynch party and tell him he's got two days to vacate."

Slocum and Jon were resetting shoes on some horses. They listened and agreed that something needed to be done. Soon the tone of things went for them to meet the next Thursday morning at the Garvin ranch. Every able man in the county was to ride up and deliver their ultimatum. He and Jon agreed to be there.

At lunch, Glenna asked him what they were going to do.

"Go over there next Thursday and tell him to leave."

"What if he won't go?"

Jon said. "They're only giving him two days."

"What then?"

"I imagine they will go back and burn him out."

Slocum agreed. "Whatever it will be, it will be final if he doesn't leave."

"Why didn't we do this a year ago?"

"Hoped it wouldn't be necessary, I guess."

"I'll be so glad to have this over."

"You won't wait long."

"Good," she said, sounding definite and putting the pot back on the stovetop.

Wednesday evening, early, two men rode into the Russell ranch to meet the "committee." By Thursday morning, men were coming from three directions, before the sun even peeped up. Rifle-armed men accompanied by the clopping of hooves, the creaking of saddle leather, and the jingle of spurs, plus a few dry coughs in the predawn. They made a circle of riders surrounding Garvin's ranch headquarters, stirrup to stirrup, in the pink first light.

On signal two shots were fired and a man with big deep voice said, "Don't shoot. We have you surrounded. Garvin, you and all your hands get out here. Come out unarmed or die."

The old man came out in his pants, and pulling up his suspenders, he looked at the crowd. "What the hell do you want?"

"If you and your men are not gone from this ranch and the area by Saturday morning, we will come and lynch each and every one of you. We didn't come to argue. You can see how many people are backing this. We will return Saturday, and if any of you are still here, be sure to wear the clothes you want to be planted in 'cause we will be back here to do that."

"You can't do that!"

"Be here and find out."

Slocum nodded to Jon, and they along with the others began to ride off—not listening to the old man's ranting and raving. He could do that until he was hoarse, it wouldn't do him any damn good—the deal was cut-and-dried.

"Will he leave?" Jon asked.

"I think so. Unless he takes his own life. He don't have much to live for losing his place."

Word went down the line. They'd ride back Saturday morning and be certain Garvin was gone. The men all agreed.

They were back at the Russell ranch by noon, and Glenna had to hear the story. They told her about Garvin's response.

Folks passing by in the next few days left word that Garvin's gunhands had all left. No one had seen him in town or leaving to go anyplace. Slocum was convinced he'd try a shoot-out with the posse and bring on his own death. But good folks could get hurt that way. Maybe some killed. Slocum didn't know any solution to the matter.

After midnight Friday, Jon and Slocum saddled up and rode cross-country to join the many others. This time each man had a rifle on his knee; before only a few had done that. They were armed for bear. They rode in silence off the rise and began to form another big half circle.

At the warning rifle shot, a man in a white shirt, unarmed, came out of the house and held up his hands. "Hold your fire, men. It's me, the sheriff. Horace Garvin hung himself last night. I came up here to check on things. I understand your concerns. Let's not let this happen again. I want law and order here. If you had reported some of the worst of these incidents I have been hearing about here at the last, I could've shut this whole thing down a long time ago, but you didn't tell me there was this kind of violence, with women raped, and . . . Let's make this a better place to live. Now, go home and hug your families. Oh yes, and thank Jon Russell and John Clark for starting this by breaking this thing and arresting the rustlers."

A cheer went up, and after shaking several hands, they rode home.

Glenna met Slocum and Jon and had lunch ready. "What now, big man?"

"Catch my mule. Load him up and head south, I guess."

"No bribing you to stay the winter?" She was holding his arm tight as they headed for the house.

"I'd love to do that, but I have an itching tells me I have been here too long."

"Then I guess we better pack you up to leave."

Jon stopped them. "Hold everything. I hate tears and gnashing teeth. I am going over and see Carter and Helen for a few days and leave you two to have your time together."

"Hey you don't have to go—" But Slocum couldn't stop him.

"Yeah, I do." With that he headed for the pen to get a horse saddled and wouldn't even stop for lunch.

"I hated to run him off," Slocum said privately to her.

"No problem. He knows how I feel about you. He's just being Jon. Jon's girlfriend died before they got married. No one has spun him around since that happened. Someday he'll find one."

"Maybe he's like you—hard to please."

"Maybe worse. If you ever get shed of this wanted business, come back to Nebraska."

"Thanks. I will consider it."

"I didn't expect you back this time and you've spoiled me."

"Me too."

He left two days later. Leading the mule and riding a stout bay horse. He wandered south by southeast. Five days after parting with Glenna, he was in York, Nebraska, headed south, when he saw a red-and-yellow painted wagon, marked WATER AND TREASURE WITCHING. Under that was this announcement: WE CAN FIND YOUR NEXT WATER WELL OR LOST JEWELRY—MURTY MCBRIDE.

He stood in the stirrups and rode hard until he was beside her as she drove her spirited horses.

"Hey, is that you?" she screeched and fell back to halt her horses. "That you under all that fuzzy face? Gods, man. Am I ever glad to see you alive. Why, there's been three bodies turned in as yours." Then she put her hand over her mouth. "I better quit shouting."

She finally sawed down her team to a stop. He dropped out of the saddle and stretched the pants out of his crotch. Then she came running into his arms.

"What about the house in Iowa?" he asked with her in his arms.

"Oh, hell, I'd have been bored to death. I can find water wells and jewelry lost. Plus it's lots of fun—folks really think I am," she wrinkled her nose, "a witch, and that gives me lots of power. I am going to a man's place today and find him where to drill for water. Go with me."

"I'm John Clark these days. Did you get all your money?"

"Did I ever. I have it so if I die my niece in Iowa is to get it or what is left. Right now I make ten dollars for finding a good well. And I average at least two to three wells a week. You need some money?"

"No, I'm fine right now."

"Come along with me today and we can have some fun after I find his well."

"Let me tie my stock on back. Where is this place?"

"There is a store out here, and he lives two miles west of there. John Jeffers is his name."

"Fine."

"Where have you been?"

"Oh, I took a herd of cattle from Wyoming to Montana."

"And you are back already?"

"Yes. I want to be in south Texas by the time the snow flies."

"Sounds like you will make it. I could witch wells down there, couldn't I?"

"You bet." His horse and mule tied to the wagon's back gate, he used his hand to boost her firm ass back up onto the wagon. She was still wearing her short dress trimmed in lace that he remembered buying for her.

They were traveling along at a good clip over the rolling prairie when the store came in sight.

"Stop," he said to her as a man on horseback out in front of the store drew his six-gun to shoot at them.

His gun blast scattered the empty-saddled horses the man was holding. Murty reined her horses out into the prairie to get out of range. Slocum, gun in his fist, jumped down and ran toward the shooter, who, in the confusion, was wound up in panicked horses. Slocum paused to take a planned shot. His bullet struck the shooter and he pitched off his horse.

As Slocum expected, more robbers came out of the store looking for him. A blaze of bullets filled the air as he dropped onto his belly and returned fire. He was under a small rise as he reloaded his six-gun, which gave him some protection. There were four other hard cases wanting to reach their scattered horses. It was everyone for his own self. One man, while on the run, was reloading his handgun. Slocum shot him in the leg.

Another man on the store porch issuing orders was silenced by a .44/40 rifle shot that Murty delivered from her wagon. Then a bareheaded man came out of the store with a shotgun. His head was bleeding, but the charge from his shotgun downed another.

Slocum was on his feet, chasing the last robber trying desperately to get on his spooked horse. When the outlaw found his stirrup to swing over, a rifle shot stopped him and he fell off. The fight was over.

Slocum saw Murty coming on the run, her bare legs showing as she ran packing the smoking rifle.

Out of breath, she asked him, "Why is that man bleeding?"

"I guess he was beaten by these would-be robbers."

"Are you all right?" she asked the shaken store man.

"Yes, now that you two have cut down these robbers."

"Well, you sure are bleeding. Slo—Clark can handle them now. Go inside and we will stitch and bandage you up some."

"Oh, you don't need to fuss over me, ma'am."

She caught his arm. "My name is Murty. Not ma'am. You may need stitches. Get inside. You have a wife?"

"No ma'am. I mean Murty."

"There ain't a doctor out here?"

"No. I'll be fine."

"My stitches may not look pretty, but that bad cut will be closed. Who were those men?"

"Some drifters, I guess." She took him inside while Slocum disarmed the wounded men and moved them closer so they could be together for him to watch them better. The man shot in the back by the storekeeper was dead.

A few farm people drove up and asked what had happened. Then they went to gather the outlaws' horses and move the dead man.

"The sheriff know about this?" one of them asked.

"It just happened," Slocum said. "We drove up and the lookout shot at her and me."

"How is Erwin?"

"Oh, Murty is in there stitching his head where they must have beat him with a pistol."

"He all right?"

"I think he will be fine."

"Can we take one of those horses and go get the sheriff?"

"My boy can ride one. He'll get the law out here," another said.

"Fine, take one," Slocum said to the second man. "Some of you watch them. I'll go check on Erwin."

They agreed as yet more came and the word spread. Slocum went inside and found Murty finishing up her work on the man's forehead.

"This iodine is going to burn, but you need it to keep down an infection," she told him.

"Oh, I'll be fine. I am so glad you two came by or I'd be dead."

"You made a good fighter and a fine patient." She kissed him on his bald head.

"Where did you learn to do this?" Erwin asked.

"Sewing up buffalo hunters and being their chief cook."

He shook his head again. "I am so lucky you two came along."

"We sent for the sheriff," Slocum told him.

"Good, he needs to clean this up. I don't know where they came from. I never saw them before."

"No matter. He can handle it."

"What can I do for you two to repay you?"

"Nothing, we will be fine," Slocum said

"I must do something. I owe you so much."

"We need to go witch a well down the road. I promised a man I'd do that today." Murty got ready to leave.

"I understand, but stop by on your way back."

"We will."

"Thanks."

It took a bit of time to drive Murty's wagon up to the house. A man came out, and she bounded down into Slocum's arms and went around back to get her peach forks.

The man's wife came out and nodded to Slocum as he stood back. "Is she for real?"

Slocum nodded. "Yes. Murty has the power to find things."

"I hope so. We've drove three sand-point wells, and they're all dry. Hauling all our water is a big pain. And that pipe is expensive."

"I know what you mean."

"You her husband?"

"No, we are friends."

"I hope she finds some water. We are thinking about giving up on our homestead if we don't find some."

Murty found no water around the home place. "Driest place I have ever witched in Nebraska," she said, raising her forks. Then she went east with the forks turned down.

"Here, there is water."

"How deep?" Jeffers asked, looking at the distance downhill to his homestead.

"There is water down there. I am not good at feet deep."

"You couldn't find any water closer?"

"No, there is none in the yard. This is where you can drive a sand point and get water."

"Can you wait while I try?"

"Sure."

He went and got a wagonload of pipe and a sand point to haul up there. He soon began to hammer the pipe down into the ground. His wife brought them sandwiches and tea while the pipe went farther down with each sledgehammer blow. New pipe connected, and he drove it deeper each time. His hard work continued. Slocum took over while he rested a bit, and finally when Jeffers went back to driving and grumbling, water began to bubble out of the pipe, and soon it showered over them in the air.

Jeffers danced with Murty and shouted. "You've done it! You've done it!"

His wife did the same with Slocum. Everyone was excited. Slocum knew Murty was excited; she was giggling like her old self. The farmer broke out some homemade wine, and they all four about got drunk over the water find.

The sheriff came by, spoke to them about the robbery, and thanked them. His men were taking the prisoners back to York. He doubted some of them would live. He also drank water from the Jeffers' new well and told them they had a good one.

Murty and Slocum stayed over the night and slept together in a bed in the wagon. She still giggled when he entered her, and they had a good time making love.

"I can't stay here much longer," he told her.

"Where will you go?"

"Wander south and keep my head down. I don't need a newspaper story that might show our being together again and bring the Pinkertons down on you."

"Gods I'd hate that."

"So would I, but facts are facts, and those outfits have you down as a person of interest, I bet."

"I never thought of that."

At dawn, he loaded the mule, saddled the bay, and rode south. Just him and the meadowlarks, darting about, and them singing songs to him. He sang some trail songs as he sat in the saddle, riding south across the country to the Republican River and crossing on the ferry. Not daring to stop and see Jenny Nelson and her boys, he rode on, trying to be as unnoticed as he could. He'd also passed the Pawnee lands north of there and kept going on his way.

Abilene was a farming town. He realized that fact, so he didn't spend any time there. A hundred miles south, Wichita was about to give up its crown as the queen of the cattle drives and move the title west on to Dodge City. He snuck in under cover of night and looked for some old friends. Lots of unfamiliar faces crowded the street, and plenty of Texas cattle were there near the end of the summer.

In the Red Dog Saloon, he slipped into a card game with two men he knew who were discreet. Alan Collins and Jasper Wentworth. Collins was the better gambler, but Wentworth had a lucky streak that evening and kept drawing good cards in the game. Slocum trusted each man to keep his identity quiet. When he took a seat and introduced himself as Clark, neither of them raised an eyebrow. The game went on.

Slocum won a little and lost some. When the game broke up and the three of them were alone, Collins asked how he had been.

"Good, but I guess Pinkerton is looking for me."

"They've been running around. We all wondered who'd swallowed you."

"I've been to Montana."

"Really?"

"Sold some high-priced cattle up there."

"Oh, it was you made that big deal for Jim Caltron? I read about that."

"You know him?" Slocum asked.

"Yeah, he was sure proud of that sale."

"What was the deal on his wife?" Slocum asked, still curious about the outcome of Caltron's return.

"Oh, he got took on her. She ran around on him, I'd bet, from the day he left. But he is divorced now and doing fine.

You need to stop by. I know Jim well. He thinks you're a real hero selling his herd for all that money."

"Good. It's nice to see both of you and catch up."

"We know you're wanted. Have they hounded you?"

"Yes. But so far that's all they've done."

"That's a tough deal. All of us heard your side of the story. Anything you need? Money?"

Slocum shook his head. "I only wanted to get in touch with some friends and learn all I could."

"They haven't given up," Collins said.

"Oh, I knew that." He laughed.

He rode south the next day. Past many herds that he knew would be wintered there because the market was so crowded by this time of year. He was deep into the Indian Territory in a few days. He knew a Choctaw woman, and he aimed to spend a few days with her if she wasn't preoccupied.

He approached Anita Strawberry's place quietly and sat on his horse in the post oak timber for several hours watching to be certain she was alone. Then, satisfied, he rode in.

"How long you been spying on me, big man?" Her smile was warm. In her early thirties, she had a willowy figure and her hair was in a single braid down her back.

"I didn't want to disturb you and some lover."

"Or one of Parker's deputies prowling around, or even a Pinkerton man asking me damn questions about you. How did I get on that list?"

"You musta tried hard. It's a long story."

"I sure never told them one damn thing. They been around here doing that for months now. Right after you escaped that bunch of lawmen. I read it in a Kansas City newspaper, and here come these bastards dressed in checkered suits and bowler hats—hell, they had to be Pinkerton men. They didn't need a damn badge they were so obvious. Well where was Slocum hiding? Who was hiding him? How you nearly killed them deputies you escaped from. I said it wasn't him. If it was, he'd have killed them." She threw back her head and laughed. "Oh, I had them going."

"You been all right?" he asked.

"No."

"What's wrong?"

"There's a band of outlaws Parker's men can't corral. The Choctaw Tribal Police can't either or don't want to. They do like the Cherokee Police used to. Avoid. You know they still do."

"What can I do?"

"You know how to stop a gang like that?"

"They're well armed and tough?"

"Oh, yes and elusive. They rape young girls at stomps, rob old people. No good for anything." She shook her head in disgust.

"Are there any honest people will help us?"

She nodded, and then, taking charge, she took him by the arm. "I will feed you and we can make up some time that I have missed not having you."

"My horse and mule?"

"They will be fine. It isn't raining or snowing on them."

They both laughed and went inside her small house. "Tomorrow night we can go to a stomp, and I will gather others that will help you," she said.

He shrugged. She'd already volunteered him to do the job. He seemed to get into the damndest deals with the most amazing women he knew all across the West. It was almost like they saved things up for him to do.

17

Folks always came early for the good places to camp at those stomps. Slocum hooked Anita's horse to a light wagon, put in her canvas shelter and some poles for cooking pots, and told her to get any food items she lacked out of his panniers. They were loaded after breakfast. The night before they'd bathed in the nearby stream, and she had shaved him afterward. Then she traded his boss-of-the-plains felt hat for an unblocked gray one she had and dressed him in a buckskin vest. It changed his appearance considerably, and he told her he even felt like a Choctaw.

She smiled and patted his shoulder. "I told you I'd hide you."

They were at the Henson Schoolhouse by midday, after talking to several others on the road. The wide valley sat surrounded by grassy hills with several strong springs. People chose their sites and set up under the pecan trees. Anita's setup was strung from trees, and the posts to support it were braced with staked ropes that could be tightened in case of rain. It was a stout camp.

She began to make donuts that emitted a strong vanilla flavor and drew many for a handout.

Women chattered and menfolk squatted on the ground at the edge of the large shade and told Slocum about the Scroggs gang.

Bennie Cross was a short man with a dark face wrinkled like an aged apple. He was very angry about this group of a half dozen outlaws who were overrunning the district's social events, like the stomps, that were intended to bring their culture back to these people.

"How can we stop them?" Cross asked, rocking on the balls of his moccasin-clad feet.

"We need bats that we can conceal beside our legs. Guns will get people killed. Then we separate them and use the bats to pick them off. After we knock them out, we tie and gag them then take them away from here and tell them the next time they will die. Separate them and let them loose in different places so they can't reunite."

"What should we do to Jim Scroggs? He is their leader and the meanest of them."

"You are the Choctaw. Do what your people expect of you. I am just a helper."

"I am grateful for what you have suggested." He nodded his head under the snap-brim hat. "We can do that. I will send others to talk to you. Separate the gang and take them out. I like that."

"They will also need rope and a gag besides the bats."

"I am sending for bats. A sawmill can make them. We will be well armed."

"Does he have spies?"

"They concern me. We will stop them."

Slocum agreed. Cross left him with a handshake, and he watched the small man shuffle away. The plan was set. He went to refill his cup with Anita's coffee and to eat more donuts. Two of her cousins were helping her cook all the donuts, which quickly disappeared.

"Well Anita is smiling today," her cousin Anna said.

He shrugged. "Maybe she smiles easy."

"She says you have plans for those bad ones."

"I hope so."

She laughed. "I hope it works. I hate them for ruining our fun and traditions like they have in the past."

"I think I came up with a plan."

She nodded firmly. Then a small boy came and made her bend over to hear his words.

She stood up after thanking him. "Come with me. Three of Parker's men just rode into camp." Without a word, she hustled Slocum out the back way. On the way out, she gave a facial signal to Anita and received a nod in understanding. Then Anna soon had Slocum in a sidewall tent. She put a colorful trade blanket on his shoulders and added a straw hat.

"Stay around here until dark. They are only checking for wanted men, people who owe fines, escaped, or did not show up for their court appearances. And to look for whiskey. They won't expect to find you here."

He thanked her and took a seat on a bench in the shade. Two men in suits rode by him on horseback, checking things as they went. They only gave him a slight glance. Neither looked familiar to him, but he only knew a handful of them. Slocum was now joined by others, and the group pretended to be gambling. One man spoke softly, "They won't arrest you."

Slocum gave him a nod. They were covering him well. Cross dropped by. He squatted down. "We think we can get Parker's men to arrest Scroggs. If they find over four gallons of untaxed whiskey in his possession, they have to take him to Fort Smith. I have a man who can water enough down to have five gallons we can plant in his camp."

"That sounds good. But will they arrest him?"

"Yes. They have to."

"Without a leader, the others may run away."

"I think so too. Stay here. You are safe here."

"Thanks."

A woman laughed as she fed him some rich beef stew. "My name is Lana. If you get tired of Anita, come see me."

By dark, he was led back to Anita's camp and wore her hat again. He noticed three bats that still smelled of being fresh-cut wood. They were square, but he figured lots were being rounded to use.

"I an sorry you had to sit alone down there," she said to him.

"Oh, I had several propositions and plenty of good food."

She looked at the ceiling for help. "No doubt my good friends."

"Cross is going to try to get Parker's men to arrest Scroggs."

She shook her head. "That won't work."

"It might."

"We will see."

She fed him her fried chicken and fresh hot biscuits with butter and blackberry jam. Her cousins were there to eat too. One of the women got up and gave a bat to a man who came by for one.

The sun was down, and drums were beginning to be beat, filling the valley with their sound.

"I think we should not be too obvious," Anita said. "No telling how many marshals are here. But we can watch and maybe help Cross with his plan."

Slocum agreed. They were in the shadows when a commotion broke out in the north part of the valley. Word soon came back that Scroggs had been put under arrest for moonshining. The news spread fast, saying that the marshals made a large show of force—expecting maybe a force to rise up to stop them. But Scroggs was quickly carried away under tight guard in a wagon for the federal jail in Fort Smith. That reduced the lawmen remaining there.

Scroggs's henchmen went about the camp growling about how they should have stopped his arrest, but no one but them missed him. They soon began heavy drinking, and the number of bat-carrying men increased. Two of the Scroggs gang started pushing people aside and calling them cowards for not stopping the law from taking their friend.

They did not leave the central part of the dancing, but men with bats at their side started to separate them from the crowd. Slocum smiled to himself.

Three of Scroggs's men were talking to some teenage girls at the edge of the firelit circle. Slocum wondered if the girls were the bait and decided they must be. He saw the pursuit and knew the Scroggs boys would soon have headaches and be bound and thrown out of the camp.

Two hours later an all-clear was celebrated. Word spread like wildfire. All the gang was gone. The last marshal had also left the camp. Slocum and Anita stomped into the morning hours. When she took a break, one of her cousins stole him to stomp with her. Their spirits were high, and the wave of fear was replaced with one of having fun.

They knew how to do it well.

Cross spoke to him briefly after midnight. "We won't forget to use bats next time. My people are in your debt."

"May the sun shine on your happiness."

"It will." Cross left him with a smile.

After a week with Anita, Slocum saddled up his horse and loaded his mule. Two days later he crossed on the Red River ferry. Many times he recalled riding back across that river headed for south Texas. The rolling grass country of north Texas spread out as he rode south in the shortening days of fall.

He moved more west to avoid Fort Worth. One night he camped on a small river well west of the city.

A man dropped by his firelight and asked to come into his camp. He wore the ten-centavo star of the Rangers on his vest.

"Evening, mister. I'm running late getting back. Glad you didn't refuse me. Some folks don't appreciate lawmen."

"Set a spell. I don't have any reason not to invite you in." He poured him some coffee. "Who are you looking for?"

"Oh, we got word some wanted guy named John Slocum was out and about Abilene."

"Was he?"

"No, the guy I found was just a drifter. My name's Sam Grove."

"John Clark. Been driving cattle north and coming back. Guess you get lots of calls that don't pan out."

"I bet this guy they are looking for is resting in an unmarked grave somewhere. He escaped some U.S. Marshals in Kansas and I bet he froze to death. No one's seen him since then."

"He might have."

"He shot some congressman's son, they said."

"Bad deal."

"Yeah, bad deal for me having to go clear out to Abilene and find some drunk drifter. Damn sure he was not Slocum."

They parted the next morning shaking hands. Grove told him to have a great trip south and to get home safe. Slocum told him to do the same.

He spent most of the warm, sunny day smiling to himself. *Slocum is somewhere in an unmarked grave.* He hoped more lawmen thought the same thing, as he booted his horse into a jog.

Watch for

SLOCUM AND THE BULLET EXPRESS

422nd novel in the exciting SLOCUM series
from Jove

Coming in April!

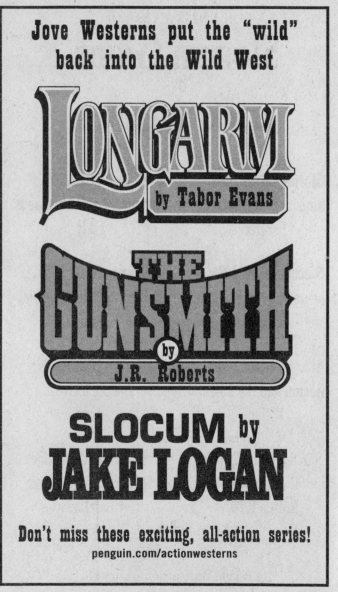